CHRISTMAS FOR A GODDESS

DRAGON LORDS OF VALDIER NOVELLA

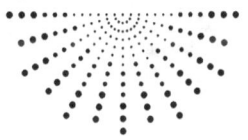

S.E. SMITH

MONTANA
PUBLISHING

ACKNOWLEDGMENTS

I would like to thank my husband, Steve, for believing in me and being proud enough of me to give me the courage to follow my dream. I would also like to give a special thank you to my sister and best friend, Linda, who not only encouraged me to write, but who also read the manuscript. Also, to my other friends who believe in me: Julie, Jackie, Christel, Sally, Jolanda, Lisa, Laurelle, Debbie, and Narelle. The girls that keep me going!

And a special thanks to Paul Heitsch, David Brenin, Samantha Cook, Suzanne Elise Freeman, PJ Ochlan, Vincent Fallow, L. Sophie Helbig, and Hope Newhouse—the outstanding voices behind my audiobooks!

– S. E. Smith

Summary: A Goddess shares a special Christmas with a human man
that gives her a gift she never expects—love.

ISBN: (Paperback): 978-1-959584-11-7
ISBN: (eBook): 978-1-959584-10-0

Published in the United States by Montana Publishing, LLC and SE
Smith of Florida Inc.

{Romance (love, family, friendship) – Action/Adventure – Fantasy –
Contemporary – Paranormal – Science Fiction Romance.}

www.sesmithfl.com

SYNOPSIS

Sometimes, even a Goddess needs a touch of magic...

Aikaterina has lived since the dawn of time. Her species was born at the same time as the universe, yet she yearns for something more. Her experiences with the Valdier, Sarafin, Curizan, and especially the Dragonlings, has left her craving something she never expected—a sense of belonging.

Bear Running Wolf is shocked when he discovers a beautiful, alien woman standing in the snow-covered woods on Paul Groves' Ranch. He knows that not all the visitors to the ranch are human... he just never expected to meet a woman from another world.

Two lonely and lost souls from different worlds have only one wish—not to be alone. Can the magic of Christmas heal them, even if it is only for a short time?

CHAPTER ONE

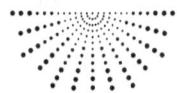

*E*arth:

Aikaterina lifted her face to the soft, fluffy flakes of snow. In her current form, she could only sense what they might feel like. Her species could take on a multitude of forms, allowing them to observe the thousands of species that lived throughout the multiverses. Currently, she was more like the mist that made up the ice crystals that coated the trees and ground than the physical form that made up humans here on Earth.

Her form shimmered, almost disappearing for a moment. She focused, pulling the energy surrounding her closer to keep from fading completely away. She was dying—at least dying in the way most species would think of it. Her kind did not think of death in the same way. They simply... no longer existed. They returned to the energy of the stars from which they were created.

I've lived for trillions of years, but it seems like a blink of an eye. There is still so much I wish to see... to observe, she reflected, gazing with appreciation at the beauty surrounding her.

She glided across the uneven, snow-covered ground, unhindered. A rabbit, sensing something unusual was in the forest, bolted across the wintery ground. The rabbit startled a young buck who stood frozen. The buck warily searched the surrounding area for any danger. A shiver caused his skin to ripple over taut muscles.

I mean you no harm.

She sent the calming waves of reassurance to the wild creature. The buck lifted his head and sniffed the air. Aikaterina materialized a few feet from the wary animal. She chose the same appearance that she used with the children of Valdier. It was a cross between the human form and the Valdier. Her complexion still had a touch of gold to it, making her skin exude a slight glow, as if she had spent a lot of time in the sun. Her hair was long, black as midnight, and fell like a curtain down her back. She wore a white gown, the same color as the surrounding landscape. A long white coat that touched the ground shielded her from the elements.

"You are a curious beast," she murmured, reaching out to stroke his forehead.

The buck rubbed his head against her hand as if in agreement. Aikaterina felt the creature shiver under her touch. It was curious... but it was also in pain. Blood seeped from a wound near its right shoulder. She ran her hand over the area, disintegrating the bullet embedded in the muscle and healing the damage it had done. The beast looked at her with wide, curious eyes, as if trying to understand who, or what, she was. She sent another wave of comfort to the buck when he nudged her with his nose as if to thank her for her help.

The snap of a branch sounded through the quiet forest and the buck restlessly stepped back, turning his head toward the direction of the noise. Aikaterina knew about the hunter's presence from the moment she appeared. She lifted her hand, sending a flurry of snow swirling into the air. The white-out concealed the buck as he escaped deeper into the woods.

~

Bear Running Wolf lowered his head and shielded his eyes from the flurry of snow that suddenly blew up in a blinding veil of white. Crouching down, he studied the speckles of blood and the deer tracks in the snow that he had been following all afternoon with growing anger. As assistant ranch foreman for the Grove Ranch, he helped keep the ranch running smoothly and safely.

Earlier there had been three separate sets of tracks, two human and the one belonging to a large buck. He had dealt with the human ones— along with the help of the sheriff. Now, he needed to see if he could help the buck.

Regret filled him. He hoped the deer's wound was minor and it would heal. His biggest concern was that the wound would lead to a slow, agonizing death.

He had just caught a glimpse of the buck when he stepped on a branch, buried under the layer of fresh snow. The loud snap made him wince. He looked up to see if the noise had startled the buck when the sudden swirl of snow obscured his view.

He lowered his head to protect his face from the frigid ice crystals. When the unexpected swirl faded, he lifted his head and scanned the snow-covered area. The scene looked like a Christmas card with the rolling slopes and snow-laden trees. The collection of Ponderosa Pine, Plains Cottonwood, Bur Oak, Quaking Aspen, Chokecherry, and shrubs all covered in snow was beautiful.

He rubbed his gloved hands together and sighed. Christmas was in two days and a foot of fresh snow had fallen last night. He had been out on his routine survey to make sure everything was good when he saw the fancy four-wheel drive GMC truck with the custom paint job along one of the fire-break roads. He knew who it belonged to—Atkins Holbert. Atkins was the son of the local bank president and the grandson of a State Representative. He was also an all-around first-class jerk who had never grown out of his high school mentality of thinking he was better than everyone else.

Atkins crossed the line when he stepped onto Paul Grove's property. There were no hunting signs posted all along the fence line and every local knew better than to step onto the ranch without first checking in with either himself or Mason Andrews, the ranch foreman. There were things—and people—that came and went on the Grove ranch that weren't meant to be seen by others.

A brief flash of pain and regret flashed through Bear. With a sharp shake of his head, he pushed the emotions away and rose to his feet. He didn't have time for distractions. He needed to find the buck and make sure that it would survive.

As he rose, a movement to his right caught his attention and his eyes widened in surprise. A woman stood in the snow. He was so surprised by the vision of her, that he lifted a hand to rub it across his eyes to see if he was hallucinating. He blinked and she was still there.

She had her back to him so he couldn't see her face. She was wearing a long white coat that shimmered in the faint, late afternoon sunlight filtering through the barren trees. The hem was decorated with thousands of tiny diamond-like crystals resembling the shapes of snowflakes. The hood of the coat was edged with soft fur. Her hands were bare and he had an insane impulse to cup them between his and warm them.

All the air in his lungs expelled when she looked over her shoulder at him with a serene expression, completely unfazed by his presence. Eyes the color of the night sky stared back at him. They were so dark, he couldn't tell if they were black or just a rich, dark chocolate. Skin, touched by the sun and as smooth as satin screamed to be caressed. Wisps of her black hair peeked out from under the white hood, creating a dramatic contrast. His gaze lowered to her lips. They were slightly parted. In the back of his mind, he registered that there was no breath-fog when she breathed.

He slowly walked toward her, afraid that she would disappear before he reached her. There was something... ethereal... about her. If he had any doubt in his mind that she might not be one of the aliens that sometimes visited the ranch, they disappeared when he looked into her eyes again and swore he could see the reflection of stars and planets in them.

"I... Mason didn't tell me that... anyone was coming to visit," he said in a voice that had grown hoarse.

The woman tilted her head and studied him a moment before she turned to look ahead of her again. He followed her gaze. His eyes widened when he saw the large buck standing a short distance away— watching them.

"The buck... I need to see if he's hurt," he said.

"He was, but he is no longer," her voice held a hint of disapproval in it that took him by surprise.

Her flashing eyes looked him over him once more, pausing on the rifle he was carrying over his shoulder. He realized that she must think that he shot the deer. He shook his head.

"I was tracking him, but I wasn't the one who shot him. Wait a minute... what do you mean he is no longer hurt?" he asked with a frown.

"That he is no longer injured. There is a sense of serenity here. I can understand why Paul, Trisha, and the dragonlings enjoy coming to this world," she murmured.

"Dragonlings... Okay, I think I missed that visit, though I remember Chad mentioning something about kids called dragonlings appearing right before his sister, Sandy, moved away," he said.

"Ah, yes. The story of the Lonely Dragon. The Dragonlings helped Sandra heal Jarak Draken's, a Valdier dragon-shifter, heart," she replied with a serene smile.

"Okay, yeah. I guess. Chad just said that Sandy met a guy she used to work with and that they fell in love and moved back to Washington, D.C.."

"Who harmed the creature?" she asked.

Bear frowned again, thrown off by the question. He looked at the buck who was moving off into the woods. Dried blood coated the buck's right shoulder.

"A guy from town named Atkins Holbert and a friend of his decided to trespass and illegally hunt. They aren't going to have a very good Christmas," he replied. "So... you are from—" He pointed upward.

She followed the movement of his hand. Her serene expression never changed. She nodded.

"Yes, I'm from... up there," she replied.

Bear's eyes remained locked on her face. He was intrigued by the slight, mysterious smile that curved her lips. Hell, he was intrigued by her lips.

"I'm Bear... Bear Running Wolf. I'm the assistant ranch foreman for Paul Grove's ranch," he introduced.

Her lips parted and she studied his face before she responded. "I am... Aikaterina."

He smiled and extended his hand. "It's a pleasure to meet you, Aikaterina."

CHAPTER TWO

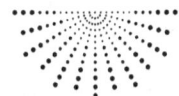

*A*ikaterina studied the human male. The only ones she had ever really interacted with were the children. She had briefly communicated with the human women, but never as she was with the human named Bear.

"Your name... is that not what one of the beasts of your planet is called?" she inquired.

He chuckled and grinned. "Yeah. Most people think I'm named after my animal spirit. In truth, my mom said she named me Bear because it felt like she was giving birth to one. I was a big baby."

She returned his smile. While she didn't completely understand everything he was explaining, she knew enough to know that his mother had a sense of humor. From his laughter and the shimmer of amusement in his eyes, he did as well.

She liked his eyes. There were a warm, rich brown that reminded her of the coloring on the buck. She held her hand out when thick, fluffy flakes of snow began to fall again. Her lips parted as the flakes collected in her hand. She had seen snow on a thousand different worlds; yet, this time seemed... different.

Surprise... another unfamiliar emotion swept through her when a warm hand covered hers in a gentle grasp. She studied Bear's large hand. There were scars on his knuckles and a place that looked like his flesh had been burned.

"You've been hurt," she said, stepping closer and lifting his hand closer to her.

"A few scrapes and burns. It comes from life on a ranch," he said.

She looked at him. "May I ask you something, Bear?" she inquired.

He released a short, sharp laugh and shrugged. "Yeah, I guess so. I'm not sure you'll like the answer if you want the truth."

"I do... want the truth."

He nodded. "Then, fire away. What would you like to ask?"

"If you had one wish, what would it be?"

He frowned and absently rubbed her hand with his thumb. "That's a bit of a loaded question. Is it like the one wish that a genie could grant, or is it one of those deep questions that people ask themselves and can never answer?"

The laugh that bubbled up from deep inside her startled her. As it grew, so did the power surrounding her until she was glowing with it. The smile on Bear's face wavered before he stared at her with a slightly awed expression. She lifted her hand until her palm pressed against his.

"That is a question I'm afraid that you will have to answer. What do you want Bear? At this moment in time?" she quietly asked.

He was silent for a moment. His gaze locked with hers until she was the one who felt as if she were falling into the depths of his eyes. Time slowed until the snowflakes fell as if in slow motion around them. Each tiny ice crystal forming its unique delicate pattern.

"Hot chocolate. Would you like some?"

She tilted her head and silently pondered his offer before she nodded. "Yes, I believe I would like to try some."

He threaded his fingers through hers and nodded back the way he came. "I left my snowmobile a short distance from here."

Aikaterina bowed her head in acknowledgement. She could have whisked them to wherever Bear wanted to go with a thought, but—

For this once, I think I would like to experience this as a human would.

Bear guided her through the thick snow. While the wide contraption connected to his boots kept him from sinking into the deep snow, she floated along the surface. He paused after they had covered a few feet to make sure she was alright, lifted an eyebrow in inquiry, but didn't say anything.

Valdier:

"Whatcha' doing, Phoenix?" Spring asked.

Phoenix looked up from the small mirror that Arilla had created and given to her. It wasn't a mirror that reflected her image, not like the real mirrors. This mirror was more like a window to the universe.

"Watching," she replied, bending her legs and crossing them.

She was lying on her bed surrounded by a dozen books. The soft patter of rain made the day a perfect day to read. She lifted an eyebrow at her sister. Spring's hair and clothing were wet. From the slight streaks of dirt still clinging to her, she must have been out in the gardens again.

"I told you it was going to rain today," she said.

Spring released an inelegant snort and shrugged. "I knew it was going to rain. It is good for my plants. I don't mind it and my dragon and Little Bit love it."

Phoenix looked over to where Little Bit, Spring's symbiot, was rooting around on Spring's bed. She rolled her eyes. The bedspread would be soaked which meant Spring would be sleeping with her tonight.

Spring was changing out of her wet clothes. She released a shriek of surprise when Alice and Adaline suddenly appeared out of thin air. Both girls giggled at Spring's startled reaction.

Phoenix rolled onto her back and shook her head at the Curizan princesses. Alice and Adaline grinned at them both. Spring picked up a pillow that Little Bit had knocked off the bed and tossed it at Alice who caught it and turned it into an oversized feather chair.

"You know there is a door, right? The polite thing to do is to knock before entering," Spring growled.

Alice gave an airy wave of her hand in dismissal of Spring's annoyance. "I'll remind you of that the next time you pop up unannounced on my balcony in the middle of the night."

Spring had the grace to look sheepish. "I thought you might like to see the night-glowing spider lilies."

Alice put her hands on her hips and scowled. "I did... until you forgot to tell me the part about how they got their names because *there were real glowing spiders in them*," she retorted.

"I like them, Spring. Spiders don't scare me. We had lots of them on the ranch," Adaline said.

Phoenix snorted. "Yeah, Spring forgot to tell mom that too when she gave her a bunch to put on the table," she replied, rolling back onto her stomach to gaze into the mirror.

"What are you so interested in, Phoenix?" Alice asked.

Phoenix scooted over when Alice climbed up on the bed next to her. She waved her hand, expanding the mirror enough to make it easier for both of them to gaze into it. The bed bounced on the other side of her and she knew that Spring and Adaline had joined them.

"I've been really worried about Aikaterina," she confessed.

"Aikaterina? Is she like Arilla?" Adaline asked.

"Yes," Phoenix replied, turning back to study the images in the mirror.

"What's wrong with her?" Spring asked with concern.

"Her colors are faded. They aren't nearly as bright as they used to be," Alice observed.

"I know. I thought... well, I thought maybe there was something I could do to help. Arilla said that she and Arosa are worried about Aikaterina as well. They said she left to check on Grandpa Paul's ranch and they wanted to make sure that everything is okay, but there was another problem that came up and they needed to leave."

Phoenix didn't add that the two younger goddesses also had to help Aikaterina to get there, or that they had asked her to keep an eye on Aikaterina while they were away helping the people of Glitter after an earthquake struck the moon where the small creatures lived. She was supposed to let them know if Aikaterina needed help.

"Hey! That's Bear! Oh, my gosh. I wish mom could see him," Adaline exclaimed in a voice filled with excitement.

"He has a funny name like Roam and Leo. He looks just like the picture you showed me, Adaline," Alice said with a grin at her cousin's excitement.

"Roam's name isn't funny," Spring defended.

Alice shot Spring an apologetic look. "Funny in a good way. I like Roam and Leo's names. They are cool."

"Oh, okay," Spring replied with an approving nod.

"Look. Did you see that?" Adaline asked, sitting up and leaning closer to the mirror.

"See what?" Spring asked, crawling over Phoenix until she was behind Alice.

"That! Her aura is changing," Alice exclaimed with growing excitement.

"I want to see," Spring said, pressing against Alice and Adaline's backs to get a better view.

"Where did Bear gooo—oh! HELP!" Adaline suddenly cried out when she tumbled forward.

Before Phoenix could warn Alice, Adaline, and her sister not to lean in too close to the mirrored image, they all tumbled forward. Phoenix scrambled to grab them, but their combined force pulled her forward as well through the magical portal Arilla had created for her, and the four girls toppled head first through the opening.

CHAPTER THREE

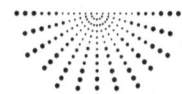

*B*ear pulled the snowmobile under the covered area next to the barn and slid off. He held his hand out for Aikaterina, and helped her off the snowmobile. He was secretly both glad and frustrated that he was wearing thick gloves to protect his hands from the frigid weather.

"You live here?" she asked, looking at the barn.

He chuckled and shook his head. "No, over there," he said with a nod toward the modest two-bedroom, one bath house he had been given to live in as assistant ranch manager.

The house looked like a rustic log cabin which he liked. There was a wide covered front porch with a couple of rocking chairs and a wooden carving of a bear. He had carved the bear out of a tree that had fallen over a few years ago. The winters could be long and lonely and it had given him something to do.

Fortunately, he had shoveled a path between the barn and the house and it hadn't yet filled in with new snow. He held her hand, suddenly aware that she wasn't wearing any gloves. With a silent curse, he tugged off his glove and wrapped his warm fingers around her hand. He was surprised that it didn't feel cold.

"Is there something wrong?" she inquired when she noticed his frown.

He studied her hand in his before he looked into her eyes with a curious expression. "You aren't wearing any gloves. Your hands should be frozen… yet, it is warm," he said.

She tilted her head and nodded. "The environment here does not affect me. Is that a problem?" she asked.

He shook his head. "No, no, it's not a problem." He looked up at the sky. The snow was falling more heavily. "I promised you hot chocolate. We'd better get inside so I can make you some."

He kept his grip on her hand. A small part of him was still afraid that she would disappear. They crossed the dug-out path that he had made earlier that morning to the steps. He knocked the snow off before cursing under his breath and turning to her.

"I'll give you a little bit of help. The steps are icy," he said.

Wrapping his hands around her slender waist, he lifted her and gently placed her on the porch. She was light as a feather, which had taken him by surprise. It was a good thing that he hadn't accidently tossed her like a bale of hay. That would have been a moment Samara would have never let him live down.

Pain flashed through him at the memory of Samara. He pulled his hands free, gripped the railing, and climbed the slippery steps, grateful for the snow cleats that he was wearing. Aikaterina touched his arm when he went to pass her.

"You feel… sorrow," she said.

He shook his head. "No. I'm just cold. Let's get inside where it's warm."

He stepped around her, used the shoe brush by the door to knock the snow off his boots, before he slipped the cleats off and opened the door. He waited until she entered before he hung the cleats on a peg.

He unlaced his boots and placed them in the rubber boot tray he used to protect the hardwood floors.

She paused and looked at the tray and his boots as he shrugged out of his heavy coat, placing his gloves on a shelf above the coat hooks to dry. He turned and studied her with an uncertain expression.

"Do you want to keep your coat on? It might be a little chilly in here. I don't usually use the central heat, just the pellet stoves for the back bedrooms and the main fireplace. They tend to do the job, but I've been gone most of the day," he said.

She looked at the fireplace. There was a stack of logs next to it, but only cold ashes in the hearth. She still hadn't removed her outer coat, so he assumed that she wanted to keep it on.

"Why don't you prepare the hot chocolate while I create a fire?" she suggested.

He frowned and warily ran a questioning glance over her pristine white clothing. Fireplaces and wood weren't known for keeping things clean. When he looked into her eyes again, he saw her amusement and he flushed.

"I'll turn up the thermostat. That will warm the place up and I can take care of the fire once I'm done with the hot chocolate. Why don't you have a seat?" he said.

A quick glance at the living room showed that it was neat. If there was one thing he had learned growing up with his grandmother, it was to always keep a tidy house. His grandmother warned him that he never knew when someone might drop by... including her.

The memory of his grandmother's lessons made him smile. Agatha Running Wolf was a powerful force to reckon with. She was currently exploring South Africa. She complained that Wyoming in the winter was too cold for her old bones.

"I don't care what misconceptions people have about Native Americans. Wyoming in winter is cold enough to freeze buffalo dung before it hits the

ground. I hate being cooped up in the house all winter. Give me hot weather and a sexy guide and I'll be happy."

He would be surprised if Agatha returned before the end of next Spring. Even if she did, she wouldn't be home long. She and her gal pals were having fun exploring the world—and he was appreciative of the privacy, especially if it meant keeping his matchmaking grandmother from trying to hook him up with every single woman between Canada and Mexico.

"Make yourself comfortable. I'll be back in a moment," he said with a wave of his hand.

She bowed her head in acknowledgement and turned away from him. He swallowed hard when she released the fastening on her thick white coat and it slid down her arms—and disappeared. If he had any doubt at all that she was from another world, it vanished as quickly as her coat did.

With a silent curse, he turned and strode through the opening into the kitchen. Glancing over his shoulder, he saw Aikaterina walking around the living room, pausing in front of the different pictures he had of his grandmother, Samara, and Adaline. There were only a couple of his mom and none of his father. His mom had left him with his grandmother when he was only a few months old and disappeared for good when he was five. His father had been gone long before his mom even knew she was pregnant.

His gaze swept over the elegant long dress Aikaterina was wearing. It was white, like her coat, but had delicate swirls of gold threaded through that looked like some kind of intricate design. The long sleeves encased her slender arms, while her midnight hair fell like a curtain down to her waist. She moved across the floor as if she were floating.

Sweat beaded on his brow despite the chilled temperature of the cabin. He flicked the thermostat on the wall to on and bumped up the temperature. Crossing over to the refrigerator, he pulled out the milk and placed it on the counter while he retrieved a pot to warm it.

He leaned his hands against the counter and shook his head. A myriad of emotions was coursing through him, making him feel off-kilter and clumsy. Pulling out his phone, he sent a swift text to Mason.

How many aliens are there this time?

He picked up the plastic jug of milk and poured some into the pot. He placed it on the stove and turned the gas on under it to low. It would take a while to heat up. In the meantime, he grabbed the semi-sweet block of chocolate from the pantry and chopped it up. Agatha never tolerated the boxed stuff. She said a good hot chocolate was made with real chocolate and love.

Memories flooded his mind of the first time his grandmother made him hot chocolate. It was the day his mom drove away. That was the last time he had ever seen his one surviving parent. Agatha had taken a very confused and angry five-year-old gently by the shoulder and began teaching him how to tame the angry bear cub that lived inside him. He picked up his phone and frowned when he read Mason's reply.

What do you mean? There aren't any here that I know of. Have you seen one?

He frowned. Paul had a strict rule that all aliens were supposed to check in with Mason first. Kelan, Paul's daughter Trisha's partner, had even set up some fancy alien communication system to make sure there were no unexpected surprises. Obviously, this alien must have missed the memo.

Yeah, I think so.

Mason immediately replied.

Whatever you do, keep them there! Ann Marie has half of her family from Colorado here for Christmas! They are not ready to know about extraterrestrial life! I told her this was a bad idea but her mother and father insisted. How many are there?

Bear grimaced with sympathy. Ann Marie's family were very superstitious and vocal about their disapproval of Mason, even after all these years. It didn't help that the elderly couple were in their late seventies and not in the best of health. The discovery of aliens and the fact that their daughter was friends with some of them would probably send them both into cardiac arrest. Something none of Ann Marie's six siblings, their partners, and her cousins would ever let her live down. He typed out a quick, reassuring response.

Only one. I'll keep her here.

Thanks. There's a storm expected tonight and tomorrow. At least that will help. Ann Marie's family is leaving the day after Christmas. If you can keep things under wraps until they leave, that would be great.

No problem.

He pocketed his phone, picked up a spoon, and slowly stirred the chocolate into the steaming milk. With Ann Marie's family here, the big house, Samara's old apartment, and Mason and Ann Marie's house would be filled to overflowing. It looked like their unexpected guest would be staying with him—winter storm or not.

Unless she beams up to a spaceship, he mused.

"May I observe you making hot chocolate?"

He turned with a smile that faltered and swallowed. There was only one thought in his head and an unexpected reaction that brought a slight coloring to his cheeks. He was glad he was wearing a sweater that was on the big side, otherwise things might get awkward real fast.

Damn but she's beautiful!

She tilted her head and a curious light shimmered in the ever-changing depths. Earlier, her eyes had been so dark, they looked like a night sky. Now, her pupils were surrounded by gold.

His eyes widened with surprise when twin gold bands on her arms moved. Mesmerized by the bands, he watched as they reformed into a different, intricate pattern that looked suspiciously like rabbits and deer.

"Uh, your... bracelets are alive," he said with a slight wave of his hand.

"Yes."

His gaze jerked up to her face at the simple response. He turned away when the rich smell of chocolate rose from the pot he had been stirring. He sensed, more than heard her walk closer. She peered into the pot.

"It smells delicious," she commented.

He released a strained laugh. "Haven't you ever had hot chocolate before?" he asked.

"No."

He stared at her, waiting for her to elaborate, but she was focused on the creamy chocolate delight. He turned the burner off and reached up into a nearby cabinet to retrieve two large mugs. He placed them on the counter along with a small plate for the Christmas cookies that Ann Marie had given him the day before.

He opened the large plastic container to reveal a delightful array of assorted chocolate chip, peanut butter, and decorated sugar cookies. He placed a dozen on the plate before resealing the container and pushing it back. His stomach growled with anticipation and he realized that he hadn't eaten since early this morning.

A soft laugh made him look up from where he was arranging the cookies. Aikaterina was studying him with an amused expression. His lips curved in a crooked grin.

"I can guarantee you've never had Christmas cookies that taste as good as these will," he promised.

She picked up a sugar cookie covered in colorful sprinkles from the plate, studied it for a moment before taking a small bite from it. He waited, watching as a succession of expressions crossed her face.

"Well, what do you think?" he finally asked, unable to wait any longer.

She held up the cookie and studied it as if it were some rare artifact. He couldn't resist. He leaned over and took the rest of the cookie from between her fingers. A soft laugh slipped from her when he moaned with pleasure.

"These will keep you from feeling hungry?" she asked.

"For a short time," he mumbled around the cookie in his mouth.

"Then... you must eat more," she encouraged.

Bear knew he should say something... agree... anything, but all he could do was stare into Aikaterina's beautiful eyes and wonder what she would say if he blurted out what he was really hungry for. Would she turn tail and disappear back to the great unknown?

Or would she fill the emptiness inside me?

He was shaken by his wayward thoughts toward a woman he had just met, along with the fact that she was an alien. Silently admonishing himself, he turned back to the pot of hot chocolate and skillfully poured it into the two mugs he had set out. He crossed to the refrigerator and retrieved the can of whip cream and added a touch to the top of each mug. For an added touch, he topped the cream with bits of the shaved chocolate he had used.

"That looks too nice to drink," she commented.

He gave her a sheepish grin. "My grandmother was all about presentation when I was growing up. It didn't hurt that I worked part-time at the local coffee shop when I was a teenager." He handed her a mug with a reindeer on it while he took the one that looked like a snowman. "With Christmas almost here, I pulled out all the punches and brought out my holiday mugs. Would you like to go into the living room? I'll get the fire going."

"I already started it," she said, taking the cheerful mug. "This reminds me of the beast from the forest... except, its nose was not bright red."

"Our deer don't have shiny red noses."

"That is a shame. I imagine it would be very helpful at times," she responded.

It took him a second to realize she was teasing him. Once again, he felt like a tongue-tied youth instead of a grown man of nearly thirty. He picked up the plate of cookies and motioned for her to go ahead of him back into the living room.

She glided across the floor. That was the only way he could describe how she moved. It was as if she floated. He knew that she wasn't. He could see her dainty feet encased in a pair of white socks when she walked.

"You didn't have to take your shoes off," he commented as they walked into the small, but airy living room.

"You did," she said.

"That's because they were covered in snow, mud, and probably a little horse or cow shit," he commented.

She sank down onto the couch across from the fireplace. He took the chair to her right, placing the plate of cookies on the coffee table in front of her first before he sat down. A frown creased his brow when he noticed that the fireplace had a healthy, cheerful fire... without any wood.

"Nice fire," he choked out, lifting his mug of hot chocolate to his lips and taking a sip.

Aikaterina smiled. "Thank you."

"So, I guess you are visiting our world. Are you one of those dragon-shifters or are you like Adalard?"

"Yes... I am... just visiting your world. No, I am... different."

He frowned. "I texted Mason. He isn't aware of your visit. Paul set up guidelines that all visitors were supposed to give us advanced warning. This is a working ranch. There are only a couple of us that know about you guys. Things can get complicated real fast if you are discovered. Is your ship hidden? It's not likely to be found between the weather and the holidays, but still, we need to take care. Ann Marie's family is in this year and they would freak out if they knew aliens existed. Where, if you don't mind me asking, are you staying?"

That same mysterious smile curved her lips. The one that hit him square in the gut and caused his groin to tighten. He tried to remember the last time he had been with a woman and couldn't. He blinked when he realized that she had spoken but he'd been so lost in thought that he missed what she said—or thought he had!

"I'm sorry. Can you repeat that?"

"I said 'I wish to stay with you'," she repeated.

"I thought that was what you said," he choked out as he sank back in his chair and wondered if the temperature in the house had suddenly risen by a million degrees.

CHAPTER FOUR

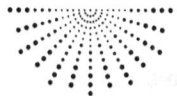

"*P*hoenix, where are we?"

Phoenix turned and looked at Adaline, Alice, and Spring. Alice and Spring had both asked the question at the same time.

"I know where we are! We're back at the ranch where I used to live with my mom," Adaline breathed in barely suppressed excitement.

Phoenix nodded and lifted her hands to the softly falling flakes of snow. "Yep, we are at Grandpa Paul's ranch on Earth."

Spring shivered. "Wel-well, I'm freezing! Even my dragon thinks this is cold!" she complained, rubbing her hands up and down along her arms.

"Here, Adaline and I can help," Alice said.

With a flick of her hands, Alice changed Spring and Phoenix's clothing. Phoenix's outfit was all in black. She was wearing thick, fluffy-lined boots, warm black trousers with a layer of shirt which was covered with a soft sweater and long wool coat. On her head, she wore a black wool knitted cap complete with a black rose.

Alice was wearing a beautiful blue gown that reached all the way to the ground and was covered by a matching navy blue coat with patterns of crystal snowflakes all along the bottom. She wore long, light blue gloves and wore an elegant light blue hat that had a long scarf that tied under her chin.

"Thank you. These are perfect!" Phoenix exclaimed, already feeling warmer.

"Oh, those are nice!" Adaline said, turning to Spring. "Let me try."

Adaline transformed Spring's clothing. Fibers wove around Spring, replacing her thin shirt and pajama trousers with layers of brilliant, thick white woolen trousers that were lined with silk and a soft, heavy knitted sweater. She added a wool and silk-lined white coat over Spring's clothes. Next, she twisted Spring's long white-blonde hair into a neat braid before tucking the soft, silky strands under a derby-style hat with a tiny blue-bird on it. A fluffy white scarf protected Spring's neck and hung down over the long white coat. Only the lower half of her legs could be seen. They were encased in white, knee-high fleece-lined boots. On Spring's hands, white gloves appeared to protect her hands from the frigid temperatures.

"Oh! This is so soft... mmm, and warm, Adaline. Thank you!" Spring moaned, burying her nose in the scarf around her neck.

"You're welcome. Now, my turn," Adaline added with a grin.

Phoenix grinned when Adaline's clothing changed into a checkered plaid shirt, blue jeans, dark brown cowboy boots, with a matching dark brown cowboy hat, coat, and fleece-lined leather gloves. She was dressed almost identically to Bear.

"Okay, so why are we here and how are we going to get home?" Spring asked.

"I don't want to go home yet! I want to see Bear," Adaline said, turning away.

Phoenix reached out, gripped Adaline's arm, and shook her head. "You can't... at least... not yet," she replied.

Adaline frowned. "Why not? He's like... right there! I miss him so much. I can tell him all about what it's like to travel on a spaceship and live on another planet... and about you guys and Alice and—"

Phoenix worried her bottom lip as she gazed at Bear's cabin. Something told her, an intuition, that they mustn't be seen... at least not yet. Her eyes widened as she had a sudden thought.

"I think I know why we are here... and I can get us home, but we have to do something first. Adaline, this is important. I need you to trust me," she stressed in a quiet voice.

Adaline's expression flickered from hope, to conflict, and finally to quiet acceptance. "Okay... but, I really want to see Bear before we go."

"I know, and you will. I promise," Phoenix said.

"Okay, so what are we supposed to be doing?" Alice asked.

Phoenix rubbed her hands together. "Not here. We need to find a spot where we can plan."

Spring looked down at the ground with a skeptical expression and shook her head slowly back and forth.

"I don't think I can dig a hole here. The ground is pretty rocky. Even if it wasn't, it's frozen. Digging through frozen ground would be really hard to do."

"I can make us a place to stay. Where do you want me to make it?" Alice asked, looking around.

"Why don't we go to the bunkhouse? It's not far from here. We could go there and plan. It's only used a couple times a year when Bear and Uncle Mason hire extra crew for the spring and winter roundups. I've only been there a couple of times, but it has a wood stove, bunks, a kitchen, and a bathroom," Adaline suggested.

"That's perfect, Adaline. Can you show us the way?" Phoenix asked.

"Yeah. It's down that road. It's not far, but it won't be easy with the snow. If we had a snowmobile, we could get there pretty fast," Adaline said.

"We don't have a snowmobile. We'll have to walk or fly," Phoenix said.

"We'd better go soon, the snow is getting heavier. I wish it snowed like this back on Valdier. Then, we'd really have a white Christmas," Adaline sighed, looking up at the sky.

"Well, whatever we are going to do, we'd better do it before our parents realize we are gone or we are going to be grounded along with the rest of the gang!" Alice said.

Phoenix silently agreed. If Mason called their moms and dads, they would be in a heap of trouble… again. At the moment, the boys were all grounded for trying to build a spaceship with Jade and Amber so they could go exploring. They might have gotten away with it if not for Jabir and Leo. Jabir had decided he needed to take some new animals back to their planet because the animals weren't happy living on Valdier.

Personally, Phoenix couldn't understand how any animal wouldn't be happy with Jabir. His parents' home in the mountains was like the coolest place to visit with all the different animals there now. It was better than any zoo.

"Okay, let's go to the bunkhouse," she said.

"It's too hard to walk in the snow. I'm going to fly," Spring grumbled as she tried to walk in the direction that Adaline had pointed.

"I wish we had brought our symbiots. They would have made this easier," Phoenix agreed.

"I could take you and come back, but it would use up a lot of energy. Adaline hasn't learned how to transport yet," Alice said, biting her lip.

"That's okay, Alice. We might need your help when we get to the bunkhouse. I know! Why don't Phoenix and I change into our dragons and you create a sleigh? Then, we could pull you. Our dragons can move across the snow better than we can," Spring suggested.

"That's a brilliant idea, Spring," Phoenix said with a grin.

"Okay. You two shift and I'll make the sleigh," Alice replied with a clap of her hands.

Phoenix stood back as Spring shifted into her dragon. While her sister looked like a white dragon, her scales had a slight tint of light pink along the edges of her scales that shimmered with color when the sun caught them just right.

Phoenix breathed, focused, and shifted next. Her dragon was different from all the other dragons. While they had scales, she had long feathers for her wings and tail. She accepted that she was different... and that her path in life would be different from those of her sister and cousins.

Her grandmother, Morian, said that she had been touched by the Goddesses. Phoenix knew that her parents worried about her. She didn't know what the future held for her, only that her connection with Aikaterina was very precious to her.

"Okay, Alice. Do your magic," Phoenix said, moving to stand beside her sister.

Alice nodded and lifted her hands. She began waving them, pulling the energy around her until she almost glowed. Adaline watched her slightly older cousin with excitement. The colors solidified, first into two long runners, then began building upward until a sleigh reminiscent of the one Santa Claus used in the picture books they had back home began to emerge.

Not to be outdone, Adaline lifted her hands and added the harnesses, complete with a row of festive silver bells, that connected the sleigh to the two dragons.

"Now all we need is hot chocolate," Adaline giggled.

"And six more dragons," Alice added with a laugh.

"Ha, ha. The boys would probably crash this thing and Amber and Jade would add booster rockets to it," Spring snorted.

"Let's go before someone sees us," Phoenix said, shaking the snow off her head. "My dragon is getting cold."

Alice and Adaline scurried into the sleigh and settled on the seat. Once they were ready, Phoenix nodded to her sister. Phoenix's dragon grunted when her front paws sank into the snow and she strained to pull the sleigh. Spring pulled hard beside her.

This much easier with Little Bit and Stardust, her dragon grumbled.

Phoenix silently agreed. If the two sisters' symbiots had been here, this would have been so much easier. Still, she was confident that between the four of them, they could accomplish the task at hand, help Aikaterina, and get home before their parents discovered them missing.

∿

Valdier Palace: Light years away

Carmen adjusted the ornament on the branch and stood back to survey the massive Christmas tree that she and Emma had been working on all afternoon. This was the last tree and was situated in the main common area where everyone would congregate in two days for this year's Christmas Eve festivities.

She looked at Emma when Emma huffed for the fifth time. A knowing chuckle slipped from her. She wondered if Emma was as worried about what the guys were up to as she was. She was about to ask when a thump outside the window made both women grimace.

"Which one do you think it was this time?" Emma asked, fighting back a laugh.

Carmen tilted her head and listened before she shook her head in resignation. "From the cursing, I'd say it was Creon."

She walked over to the window and opened it. Lying on his back on a pillow of symbiot, she peered down at him, then up at the roof of the palace, and back down again with a raised eyebrow. He grinned up at her with a wry smile and shook his head.

"Don't ask," he muttered.

"You guys aren't having a Christmas lighting contest again this year, are you?"

He shook his head. "No, this year we are actually working together. Riley threatened to skin us all alive if Vox got hurt. She said there was no way she could handle Roam and the twins on her own—well, at least, Roam and Pearl. Sacha seems to be the level-headed one of that trio."

Carmen scoffed. "Sacha is the brains behind the terrible duo. So, what are you guys doing?" she inquired, leaning against the window sill.

"We… namely Trelon and Cara… are trying to create snow for the kids. The weather is going to be chilly, but not cold enough to snow and since Mandra refuses to host this party at his mountain house until he rehomes those new beasts that Ariel rescued, we are stuck here. We want the kids to have a white Christmas, so… we are trying to make a white Christmas. Thanks for the cushion, Harvey," he muttered, rolling off the symbiot.

Harvey reformed into a werecat and snickered. Something told Carmen this wasn't the first mishap of the day. Harvey bent his front legs down, lifted his rump, and stretched before giving her a sharp-tooth grin as if in acknowledgment.

"How is the snow-making going?" Emma asked, leaning out the window beside Carmen.

Creon grimace and looked up. "It turns out Trelon and Cara are very good at making ice." He looked at both of them and grinned. "It is a work in progress."

Emma laughed. "Have you seen Alice?" she asked.

Creon lifted a shoulder. "I think she is with Phoenix and Spring. Spring got wet earlier... before the ice catastrophe. She asked where the girls were and I told her they were in their room."

Emma breathed a sigh of relief and smiled. "Thanks."

"No problem. I'd better get back up there. I think I hear Ha'ven making suggestions," he replied before shifting into a midnight black dragon and lifting off.

Carmen closed the window and studied Emma's relieved face. "What's the matter? You've been distracted all day."

Emma sighed and picked up several ornaments, fingering them as she gazed around the elaborately decorated room. Carmen could tell that something was still bugging Emma.

"It's just... well, the kids were really into the story last night and...," she began.

Carmen's breath swished out of her lungs as she finally understood what was bothering Emma. She thought of the story that Cara had shared last night. Cara's retelling had been very elaborate as she had turned the underground amusement park she had built under the palace into a winter wonderland complete with Scrooge village. They had journeyed through the theme park with the ghosts of Christmas past, present, and future as their guides.

A shudder ran through Carmen. "I think the kids have outgrown *believing* that the stories are real. They are teenagers now. I'm sure everything is fine. Creon said Alice was just going to hang out with Phoenix and Spring. With the weather being... unpredictable, they will probably be chilling the rest of the night in their rooms or head down to the amusement park. At this age, it isn't 'cool' to hang with their parents," Carmen added.

Emma sighed again. "I know. Sometimes I wonder if Ha'ven and I should have had more children, but after Ha'ven saw what it was like for me to go through childbirth, he swore he'd never put me through that again. I have to admit I am happy with only Alice. I would have been more reluctant if she hadn't had all of the other kids to grow up with and now with Adaline, it is as if she has a sister," she confessed.

Carmen chuckled. "Creon was the same. I'm happy with just the two—especially after seeing what Riley and Cara are going through," she snickered.

Emma burst out laughing. "Oh, yeah," she agreed, picking up some garland. "I'll worry about something else."

"Yeah, like what are the other kids getting up to!" Carmen laughed.

CHAPTER FIVE

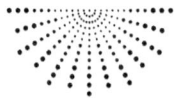

*B*ear pulled out the ingredients to make dinner. He paused, looking at the ground beef before he put it back in the refrigerator and pulled out the mushroom ravioli. He didn't know if Aikaterina was a vegetarian or not.

What did aliens eat? he mused.

Whatever they ate, it was probably not a good idea to make his world famous, award-winning chili. It was known as the best chili in Casper, but could on occasion leave behind some cosmic emissions. He wasn't so worried about himself as he was how it would affect Aikaterina.

The mushrooms sound wonderful. I would not care to eat your beast. You should know that it is not necessary to feed me, though. My kind does not require food to survive.

Bear stiffened in shock, dropping the package of mushroom ravioli on the counter. Aikaterina was in the other room, exploring the cabin which wouldn't take her long. The voice he heard was in his head. How could she know what he was thinking… unless—

Can you do that weird mind-talking stuff like Adalard and Samara do?

Yes. Though, I do not consider it weird. I know your species do not talk to each other this way, but humans have the brain capacity to evolve further.

If we don't kill ourselves first, he mused.

"You may come close, but there is always hope," she said from the doorway. "I like your home."

"Thank you," he replied.

The smile on his lips faded. He stepped toward her, stopping less than a foot from where she was standing next to the short bar that separated the kitchen from the living room. He lifted his hand and tenderly brushed a strand of her hair back.

"Where are you from?" he asked.

His voice was low as he fought with an unexpected emotion that he hadn't felt since— The memory jolted him. Breathing deeply, he shook his head and turned away.

"Samara is happy with Adalard. They were destined to be together," Aikaterina said.

Resentment flashed through him that she was intruding in his mind. He whipped around as anger course through him. The last thing he wanted was anyone, much less some alien woman he was unexpectedly attracted to, rooting around in his personal thoughts.

Aikaterina stepped back as if in surprise. Remorse filled him that he had scared her. He wasn't the kind of guy to take his anger out on a woman. He opened his mouth to apologize when her words struck him dumb.

"You… are attracted to me?" she inquired.

He lifted his hand to his face and ran it down it. He shook his head and chuckled. Turning away from her, he released a long breath.

"Yes. You are a very attractive woman and… well, let's just say it has been awhile since I've found a woman who has captivated me. It might be best if you don't go poking around in my head," he suggested. "Would you like to help me make dinner?"

"Yes."

He looked at her over his shoulder and sighed when she stood looking at him with a curious expression. He motioned for her to come stand next to him. She glided over to him and stood close enough that it felt almost like an electrical hum was pulsing off her.

"You can wash, halve, peel, and thinly slice the shallot while I get the water for the ravioli going," he instructed.

He placed the shallot on a wooden cutting board along with a sharp knife. Bending down, he retrieved a large pot, filled it with water and a dash of salt, and placed it on the gas stove to boil. Next, he pulled out the kale and minced garlic he had purchased the day before from the refrigerator. He placed it on the counter next to the cutting board. A frown creased his brow when he noticed Aikaterina staring at the shallot with a puzzled expression.

"Is something wrong?" he asked.

She looked at him. "Yes… and no. I could simply do as you ask with a wave of thought, but I… wish to do it the way you explained."

Understanding dawned and he shook his head. "Have you never cooked before?" he curiously asked.

"There is no need," she replied.

"I'm not sure I want to know what you mean by that. I know that there is one of those fancy replicator things up at the main house, but it isn't the same as fresh cooked food," he commented, not wanting to think about her earlier comment about not needing to eat. What kind of living creature didn't need food of some kind? Hell, even plants need some nutrients!

"Let's start with cutting the shallot in half," he said.

He stood beside her and picked up the knife. With a motion of his hand, he showed her how to hold it before he slid the handle into hers.

He placed the shallot in front of her and pantomimed cutting it in half with the knife. Aikaterina followed his motion, slicing through the shallot.

"Like this?" she asked, looking up at him.

Bear swallowed and nodded. "Yeah, like that. Now, gently peel the outer skin away. That's it." He took the discarded outer layer and placed it in the compost bin. "Now, slice it into thin layers. No, like this."

He moved behind her and placed his hand over hers. Electricity ran up his arm and he swore he could feel the jolt all the way to his toes. He gritted his teeth and forced his hand to move. Together, they sliced half of the shallot into thin layers.

By the time they were done, he had a thin film of sweat beading his brow. *When in the hell did cooking turn into erotic foreplay?* he wondered.

Every inch of his body was on fire. He couldn't remember ever wanting a woman as much as he wanted this one—not even Samara. The thought of Samara was like a cold shower. He released Aikaterina's hand and stepped away.

"Why don't you let me finish this? You could set the table, if you don't mind. The plates are in the cabinet above the dishwasher and the silverware is in the drawer next to the sink," he said in a strained voice.

"I can do that. I have seen the dinners the Valdier have given," she replied.

Bear silently cursed as he finished preparing their simple dinner. He didn't know if she found him attractive or not. Hell, he didn't know if they were even biologically compatible. His gaze flickered over her as she moved back and forth between the kitchen and the small, four-person dining room table in the nook attached to the kitchen.

She is so damn beautiful! he thought, pulling his gaze away to focus on what he was doing.

Ten minutes later, he placed two bowls containing the mushroom ravioli and kale on the table, along with some crusty garlic bread. He hoped she wasn't a vampire or anything. It would be very embarrassing to kill her off—not to mention hard to explain to Mason and whoever came looking for her.

"This smells delicious," she said.

"Thank you. Would you like some wine to go with it? I have some white wine that Ann Marie and Mason gave me."

"That would be lovely," she responded.

He crossed the kitchen and retrieved the bottle of Sauvignon Blanc and two wine glasses. He paused and ordered Google to play some Christmas music before he returned to his seat. Outside, the snow was falling heavier. Between the snow, the music, the delicious aromas of their dinner, and the beautiful woman sitting across from him, Bear could almost imagine what it would be like to have a real White Christmas where he wasn't alone. It's a shame he didn't have any Christmas decorations put up. He had given up on decorating after Samara and Adaline had left. There wasn't any reason to do it just for himself.

"Tell me about you," he quietly requested.

"What would you like to know?" she asked.

He thought about it for a moment before he shrugged and picked up his glass of wine. "Everything."

She laughed and lifted her glass. "That might take a few millennia. I will try to condense my existence down to a manageable timeline."

He laughed and touched his glass to hers. "Sounds good. I'm all ears."

"My existence began at the same time as the universe...."

Phoenix searched the cupboards in the kitchen of the bunkhouse for food while Adaline and Spring collected wood from the pile outside. Alice danced around the inside, waving her hands and changing the interior into a festive, comfy home that suspiciously resembled her bedroom back on Valdier when she stayed there.

"We are never going on an adventure without Little Bit and Stardust again. This is hard work," Spring complained as she and Adaline entered through the front door.

Adaline laughed. "This is all part of the fun, Spring. If you live on a ranch, you've got to get used to work," she stated as she dumped her pile of logs next to the cold fireplace.

Spring placed her logs next to Adaline's and raised an eyebrow. "Yeah, well, hard work is highly overrated. Plus, we need a lot more than the eight measly pieces of wood we carried in to get this place warm," she pointed out.

Adaline wiggled her nose. "Yeah. I guess you're right," she said.

Phoenix looked up in time to see Adaline wave her hands. A second later, a wood pile half the size of the fireplace appeared with a nice stack in the center of the fireplace. Spring shifted into her dragon and blew a stream of super-heated dragon fire at the pile of logs in the hearth. The fiery blue dragon fire quickly ignited the logs. Spring shifted back into her two-legged form and placed her hands on her hips.

"See, wasn't that a lot easier?" Spring said.

Adaline rolled her eyes. "Is there anything to eat? I'm getting hungry."

Phoenix nodded. "Yeah, there are beans and something called beanie weenies and all kinds of soups," she replied.

Spring and Alice both groaned.

"That doesn't sound very good," Spring mumbled.

Phoenix snorted. "It's better than the worms you used to eat," she retorted.

"Ew! I like beanie weenies. They are beans with hot dogs," Adaline said with a wiggle of her nose.

Spring stuck her tongue out. "I was young... and they weren't that bad. At least, I don't think dogs taste good!"

"Phoenix, can you warm some of the food up and then tell us your plan? Remember, we've got to get home before our parents know we're missing," Alice reminded her.

"And Christmas! I don't want to miss Christmas," Spring added.

Phoenix nodded. "Okay. Spring, you warm this can up while I find some bowls."

Phoenix tossed her sister a couple of cans of the beanie weenies. Spring caught them in midair with a grin. In seconds, she had shifted into her dragon form again and was gently heating the bottom of the cans, holding the heated feast between her claws so as to not burn her paws. Once she was done, she set them down and Alice removed the lids.

Adaline found some bottles of water and flavoring for them in the pantry. She placed them on the long coffee table by the fire before creating thick, plush pillows for them to sit on. Phoenix decided that having Alice and Adaline with them might be better than having the symbiots.

"We'll have a picnic dinner," Adaline said, picking a brown pillow with horseshoes on it.

"Here's a battery lantern. We can use it instead of the regular lights. I figure we don't want anyone to know we are here," Alice said.

Spring snorted. "I think the smoke coming out of the chimney might be a giveaway for that," she said, picking a fluffy pink pillow.

"Maybe with the weather, no one will notice," Phoenix commented.

"These beans aren't bad," Spring said with a grin, spooning a second huge helping into her mouth.

"I told you," Adaline laughed.

"So, what is your great idea, Phoenix?" Alice asked.

"Well, you all saw how Aikaterina's colors are fading," Phoenix explained.

"Yeah, but they grew brighter when she was with the man," Alice said with a frown.

"Exactly! Just like our mommy and daddy's do when they see each other," Adaline said around a mouthful of beans.

"Yep. Just like when our parents are with each other. It's because they love each other," Phoenix pointed out.

Alice frowned. "Okay, but what does that have to do with Aikaterina and the human?"

"Bear." Adaline muttered before she paused and looked at Phoenix with wide eyes. "Are you saying you think Bear and Aikaterina might fall in love?"

Phoenix nodded. "Why not? I mean, Arosa fell in love with the King of Glitter. Why can't Aikaterina fall in love? If it makes her better, that would be a good thing."

"I'm not sure that's how falling in love works, Phoenix," Spring said with a doubtful expression.

Phoenix leaned forward. "We've got to try. She's fading, Spring. Maybe if someone loved her like Daddy loves Mommy, she would get better. It helped Mommy when she was sad."

Phoenix bit her lip as she thought about how sad their mom had been before she met their dad. A shiver ran through her as she remembered the vision she'd had when she had visited Earth once before.

Sometimes when she visited places, she could 'see' what had happened in them. In that vision, they had been in Miss Sandy's house that had once belonged to their mom. Tears burned her eyes as she remembered seeing her mom in another life, happy with another man before she had met their father. That happiness had turned to a sorrow so deep that Phoenix knew her mother had come close to ending her life. If it hadn't been for her mom seeing Phoenix —

Phoenix looked across the table at her sister. If not for Aikaterina's touch that day, she and Spring would not be here.

"Phoenix... Are you okay?" Alice asked.

Phoenix blinked and nodded. "We need to give Aikaterina a reason to live. I think Bear could help her. If they fell in love, his love could heal her like Daddy's did Mommy," she said.

"My mom, too," Alice quietly agreed.

"But, Bear loves my mom. How are we going to get him to unlove her and fall in love with Aikaterina?" Adaline asked.

"By visiting Bear and Aikaterina like the ghosts visited Ebeneezer Scrooge," Phoenix said with growing excitement.

"But... but, he was mean and bad. Bear isn't mean or bad like Scrooge was. Neither is Aikaterina," Adaline said.

"I know, but maybe if we show them what Christmas really means, about family, love, friendship, giving, and show them how much happier they can be, they will fall in love," Phoenix said.

Adaline thought about it for a minute before she nodded. "I want to be Christmas Past—at least for Bear. I want him to remember all the good times we had," she said.

"I can be Christmas Past for Aikaterina, but I'll need some help," Spring offered.

"I am so Christmas Present," Alice said with a wave of her hand, transforming the living room until it looked like the festive halls back home.

Spring and Adaline jumped up with delight at the huge Christmas tree that took up a third of the room. Adaline waved her hand and a train appeared under the tree, complete with a tiny puffs of smoke coming from the little steam engine.

"Man, I wish we were Curizan. It would be so cool to be able to do things like this," Spring moaned.

"It's cool, but you, your dragon, and your symbiot are pretty cool, too," Adaline said, wrapping her arm around Spring's waist and laying her head on her shoulder.

"I'll be the ghost of Christmas Future, then," Phoenix stated, rising to her feet from the plump purple pillow she had been sitting on.

"When do you want to do this? Tomorrow is Christmas Eve. We have to be home later tonight or our parents are going to be furious," Alice warned.

"The ghosts visited Aikaterina... I mean Scrooge on Christmas Eve night. I think we should do it tomorrow night," Spring suggested.

"We're going to need help," Phoenix said.

Alice and Spring looked at each other and grinned. "Jail break?" they asked at the same time.

Phoenix laughed and nodded. "Yep. We need to let the others know what we are doing. We're going to need your and Adaline's talents, Alice."

Alice laughed. "Well, we have a base of operations here. Adaline and I can handle sneaking everyone out if you can get us back and forth," she said with a mischievous grin.

Adaline sighed. "I love being a part of this family," she said.

"Dragonlings totally rule," Spring agreed, hugging Adaline.

CHAPTER SIX

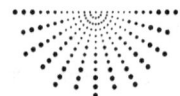

"I can't even begin to wrap my head around who... or what you are," Bear confessed.

An unexpected pang of regret swept through Aikaterina. They had moved from the dinner table to the living room again and were sitting at an angle from each other. He in the oversize plush leather chair and she on the couch across from the fireplace.

Bear had added wood to the fire, though she could have told him it would have continued burning if he hadn't. A sudden wave of fatigue swept through her and she briefly closed her eyes as it drained her. It was as if his disbelief and hesitation cut through the energy around them, sucking it away from her until there was... nothing.

"Hey, are you okay?"

"Yes... and no."

"What does that mean?" he asked.

She paused and studied his face. How did she tell him that her time was limited? He made her want things she had never imagined. For the first time, she realized that her existence had been about observing others... not truly living.

When she was with Bear, he made her feel alive in a way she had never before experienced. The power that was inside of him and that surrounded him energized her. Yet, when he looked at her with that wary expression, he also had the power to pull the fragile living energy away, leaving her feeling... hopeless.

"It is nothing. What is it you are having difficulty understanding? You have met other aliens before. You know that life exists outside of your planet... your star system."

He nodded. "Yeah, I realize that. It's that you... or your species can live so long. A human life isn't even a blink to you," he said.

"That is true, but your lives are so full. Mine suddenly seems... empty in comparison," she replied, looking down at her hands.

"My life has been pretty empty."

She looked up at him with a frown. "You are thinking of Samara again."

He flicked a quick glance at the framed picture on the mantle above the fireplace. She followed his gaze. Regret filled her along with a sense of loss.

"My species has an agreement not to interfere in the lives of the species we meet. I was dying when I traveled to the Valdier planet. My life force... was spent from my travels. I had been seeking a newly formed world where I could rejuvenate. On Valdier, there was an energy that I had not felt in a long time. I found peace." She paused and he nodded for her to continue. "I was fascinated by the dragon-shifting inhabitants there, but they were dying as well. Their dragons and two-legged form were susceptible to many diseases. I soon realized that my blood created a unique symbiotic relationship with them. I had never before found a life form that was compatible with my species. The fire within the dragons merged with my energy. In return, I also discovered the essence from both the Valdier's two-legged and dragon forms fed me in a unique way. It gave me the energy I needed not only to live, but to multiply."

"What do you mean? Multiply?" he asked.

A serene smile curved her lips and her eyes softened at the memory. "It was perfect for *my* young. I was once again strong enough to share my essence and create more of the energy that makes up my species. I am one of the ancients. I have the power to create more of my kind."

Bear frowned. "Are you saying you have... kids?" he asked.

She laughed. "Not in the way you think of children. They are created from my blood, just like the symbiots are."

"This is what I can't wrap my head around. How old you are, the way you look so... human. Or, how insignificant you must think we are," he said.

She closed her eyes and bowed her head. It was impossible to ignore the wariness and doubt in his voice. Pain pierced her when she briefly touched his mind. He found her—strange.

She opened her eyes, wondering how much time had passed because he was now kneeling in front of her. Her breath caught in wonder at the warmth of his hand against her cheek. A spark of energy radiated outward from his palm, reenergizing her.

"Bear... I want you to see me... as a... woman," she hesitantly confessed.

He tenderly caressed her cheek. In all the millenniums that she had observed the various species, she had never wondered what it would be like to be with another being... until now. She turned her face into his palm and pressed her lips against his flesh. Energy coursed through her. His emotions flowed through Aikaterina gave her an understanding of what she was experiencing.

His breath caught and he slid his hand back until he could thread it through her hair. She turned her face to his when he leaned forward and tilted her head. Her eyes locked with his in a silent question.

"Are you sure about this?" he asked.

"Very," she responded.

She met his lips when he closed the hair's breadth separation between them. Her lips parted under his and power surged through her with such an intensity that her eyelids fluttered closed. She wanted more.

She ran her hands along his arms to his shoulders then up along his face so that she could bury her fingers in his long, black hair. He moved, pressing her back against the couch. She fell to the side, pulling him down over her.

He hissed when he pulled back and stared down into her glowing face. His expression changed slightly as he looked to the side with a frown. She caressed his face.

"What concerns you?" she asked.

He blinked as if trying to clear his vision before he shook his head. "It felt... as if the world shifted for a moment," he confessed.

She leaned closer to him and whispered near his ear, "It did."

Later that evening, Bear stood in his bedroom upstairs and wondered if he was going crazy. What the hell was he thinking when he kissed Aikaterina?

"Obviously I wasn't," he muttered.

He stared out at the falling snow with growing unease. Ever since Samara left, he had guarded his heart with great caution. He had loved Samara and Adaline, and a day didn't go by that he didn't think about them and missed them.

He sat down on the chair by the window and picked up the frame with the picture of the two most important women in his life besides his grandmother. He ran his thumb over the picture of Samara smiling back at him.

"What would it have been like if you had stayed? We could be celebrating Christmas downstairs, with a big tree in front of the window, snowmen outside waiting for Santa, wrapping presents for Adaline... and maybe her little brother or sister," he murmured.

He had known Samara forever, falling for her in high school. He hadn't cared what her brothers did or her family's reputation. All he cared about was protecting her... and later Adaline. When she had moved away, it had broken his heart, but he thought if he was patient, she would come home. Everything was alright until Adalard Ha'darra, an alien prince showed up and took his hope and dreams of a life with Samara and Adaline away to a far-off world.

"Adaline would not have been safe on your world, Bear. No matter how hard you tried, another human like Alberto Frank, Armeni Campeau or General Hamade Dos would find her. Samara and Adaline are safer on the Curizan homeworld."

Aikaterina's soft voice pulled him out of his chair and he stared back at her. Anger at her intrusion fought with need. He didn't want to be alone, yet none of the women he had met since Samara left interested him—until now. He realized what he was feeling was frustration on both a physical and mental level.

"I know. I was there when both men tried to hurt them," he retorted.

He placed the framed picture of Samara and Adaline back on the antique tea table in front of the window. Shoving his hands in his pockets, he fought the urge to stride across the room and wrap them around Aikaterina.

Damn it. I can still taste her on my lips, he silently groaned.

Aikaterina's lips twitched and he knew she must have been reading his thoughts. A devilish feeling swept through him and he embraced the earlier memory of when they had kissed. He focused on all the sensations that had left him staggering for control.

Her eyes widened and her lips parted as he remembered the silky feel of her skin beneath his hands. The fire that had built inside him as he caressed her cheek before threading his fingers through the feathery-light strands of her hair. How he imagined wrapping the long strands in his fist and holding her as he buried himself inside her. He imagined kissing her again and again and again until they were both trembling with need. He would drink her intoxicating ambrosia until he was drunk with desire.

"Bear…" she breathed, stepping into his bedroom.

He shook his head. "Don't! If you come in here, if you intrude on my thoughts, then you need to know what might happen. It's been… a while since I've been with a woman, Aikaterina. I don't want—"

He bit off the last words. What didn't he want? Her? A chance of forgetting for a night everything that could have been? She deserved more than that! Any woman did. He wasn't the type of guy who would use a woman just to forget or to ease his loneliness. When he was with a woman, he wanted it to be with the understanding that they were both there for the same thing—to scratch an itch and move on.

"Humans are very complex. I have watched over your species from many different multiverses and each time I come away more fascinated and curious." She walked across his room to stand in front of him. Lifting her hand, she tenderly caressed his cheek. "You experience so many emotions that I want to feel."

"I can't promise you forever," he warned, lifting his hand and laying it over hers.

She gave him a sad smile. "I've had forever, Bear. It is not as exciting as you might think."

There was a catch in her voice and a sadness in her eyes that confused him. He wanted to wipe both of them away and replace them with hope and joy. He tenderly drew her into his arms, relishing in the way her body melded against his six foot one frame.

"Tonight, I'll do everything I can to make you feel that excitement," he promised, capturing her upturned lips.

CHAPTER SEVEN

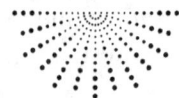

*P*hoenix silently counted everyone in the living room of the bunkhouse early the next morning. The only ones missing were Jabir and Bálint. Alice and Amber had both gone earlier this morning to get them. Phoenix wasn't sure what was taking them so long.

"Phoenix, I've got an incoming signal," Jade hollered above the noise of the excited chatter from the other dragonlings and looked over the top of the screen she was holding.

Phoenix nodded and hurried outside the bunkhouse. It was easier to create a large portal outside where there was more room than inside where it was crowded. Her body shimmered as she shifted into her dragon form. She was more powerful in this form when opening a portal. The other dragonlings hushed and spilled out of the bunkhouse behind her.

She rose into the air and focused on the connection between Earth and Valdier. The atmosphere flickered and changed as a portal opened. Soon, the darkness of space brightened until the space reflected a mirror of where Alice, Amber, and the two boys were shone as if they were looking through a window.

"Oh, no, they did not!" Spring groaned.

Oh, no, was right! Phoenix agreed.

The first thing that came through the portal wasn't any of the dragonlings, but eight of Jabir's beasts that had caused the others to get into trouble! Phoenix rose higher as the large, hairy beasts bowed their antler-topped heads and jumped through the opening. The creatures verged with four going to the right and four going to the left. The large harnesses around their necks jiggled as the silver bells attached to them announced their arrival. A few seconds later, Jabir and Bálint jumped through followed by Alice and Amber.

"Jabir!"

The chorus of groans from the other kids rose above the clatter of the reindeer-like beasts who were pawing at the snow and curiously sniffing the ground. Phoenix closed the portal and landed, shifting back into her two-legged form as she did. She placed her hands on her hips and glared at the four new arrivals.

"Alice!" she snipped.

Alice raised her hands. "Don't blame me. I told Jabir and Bálint not to bring them," she said with a huff.

"Phoenix, they'll be good. Dad was upset because they didn't like the new enclosure that he and Asim built for them. Mom says they have to stay in the barn if they aren't in the enclosure, but they were scaring all the other animals," Jabir explained.

"And you thought bringing them here would be a good idea?" Spring demanded.

"I think they are pretty cool," Roam said.

Spring whipped around and scowled at Roam. "Of course, you do! You don't *think* about all the problems that can result!"

"Well, it isn't like I can fly like you guys or just pop up wherever I want. I could ride one of these and keep up," Roam snapped.

"You don't have to! Your cat can walk in snow without sinking into it and you don't have to worry about keeping up because we wouldn't leave you behind," Spring retorted.

Phoenix knew if she didn't do something soon, that her sister and Roam would be in a wrestling match. The last thing they needed to add to the confusion was the smell of burning cat hair! She breathed a sigh of resignation and turned to Bálint and Jabir.

"You two keep an eye on… these things," she ordered with a scowl.

"Are the others good with the plan?" Phoenix asked.

"Yep. Morah is bossing everyone around. Hope, Leo, and Pearl are going to run interference while James and Sacha are operating the holograph AIs that Jade and I created so it looks like we are still there," Amber said.

"I really hope this works or we are going to be grounded forever," Zohar muttered.

"Don't fret, Zohar. Jade and I are always in trouble. It isn't so bad. Your folks will get so tired of you always moping around or being under their feet that they'll do anything to get you out of the house," Jade added.

Zohar rolled his eyes and muttered more dire predictions resulting from their current escapade. Phoenix fought a grin when Adaline snickered at Zohar. He shot the two of them a dark scowl which only made it funnier.

"Okay, let's go inside—except for Jabir and Bálint," Phoenix instructed.

"I told you they wouldn't be happy," Bálint muttered to Jabir.

"I don't care. The Poro love it here. Look at the way they are rolling around," Jabir defended.

"I really hope this doesn't turn out to be one of those invasive species things," Jade said with a shake of her head.

"It better not or I don't care how much we drive our parents crazy," Amber muttered.

"Everything will work out," Phoenix assured them with what she hoped sounded like confidence.

"So, what's with all the secrecy?" Amber asked, flopping down on the couch in front of the fireplace.

"We're going to save Aikaterina. Her aura is fading," Phoenix said.

"And help my friend Bear," Adaline added.

Jade and Amber nodded and looked at each other. "Operation Christmas for a Goddess?" Jade suggested.

"Sounds good to me. We're in!" Amber said with a grin. "What's the plan?"

Phoenix breathed out a long sigh. "Do you remember the story your mom told us the other night?"

"Yeah, but what does that have to do with Aikaterina? She's good, isn't she?" Amber asked.

"Maybe this Bear guy is mean," Zohar replied.

"No, he's good. He's just lonely since my mom and me left," Adaline interjected.

"Nobody is bad or mean. We just need to show them they would be happier together. If we can heal Bear's heart and help him get over his past and show them both that if they fall in love then they have a lot to look forward to in the future then that will help save Aikaterina and mend Bear's broken heart," Phoenix patiently explained.

"Ugh! Why can't it be cool like in the story. I could really get into being the ghost of Christmas Future. I'd be all bloody and gory," Roam groaned, rolling out of the chair onto the floor.

"If you don't shut up, I'm going to make you that way," Spring growled.

"I'd like to see you try," Roam retorted, giving Spring a sharp-tooth grin of encouragement to try something.

Amber and Jade looked at each other and rolled their eyes. "What do you want us to do?"

"Did you bring the items I asked for?" Phoenix asked, ignoring her sister and Roam for the moment.

"Yep, and a few other cool things we thought might come in handy," Amber replied holding up a large bag.

"Cool. Now, let's get planning. We only have a few hours," Phoenix said.

Bear studied the peaceful face of the woman lying next to him. Last night had been... incredible. There was no other way to describe it. He lifted his hand to move a swathe of her hair that had fallen across her face, paused and closed his eyes as he remembered doing the same thing last night, and silently cursed.

He carefully rolled out of bed and strode to the bathroom. Pausing in front of the sink, he stared into his reflection in the mirror and cursed again.

What were you thinking? You know better than to get involved with a woman like Aikaterina!

Last night had been mind-blowing. Who was he kidding? It was more than that. She had not only penetrated the wall he had built around his heart; she had obliterated it.

"One night is not going to be enough," he muttered, as he brushed his teeth.

But... how many more could they have? He turned his back to the mirror. Walking over to the shower, he turned it on and stepped in before the water warmed up. Icy streams of water struck his heated flesh, causing a sensation much like he imagined a rain of sharp needles would feel. He gritted his teeth and forced his body to remain still as the first hint of warmth finally flowed from the nozzle.

He soaped down and rinsed. He washed the scent of her from his skin, but not even the icy water was enough to erase the memory of holding her, loving her, or connecting with her on a level he had never felt before with another woman. Nothing was helping to calm his tortured mind.

Not even the memory of Samara.

Of course, he and Samara were never together the way he and Aikaterina were last night. He had always imagined it would have been similar, but now he wasn't sure. With Samara, he had always felt... comfortable. He enjoyed her wit and her sense of humor and... well, there had been an overriding need to protect her from her crappy brothers.

With Aikaterina—

He pressed his hands to the shower wall and bowed his head so the water would run over the taut muscles of his shoulders. Closing his eyes, he tried to stop the memories of making love to Aikaterina and the way she fit so perfectly in his arms as if they were made for each other.

A low moan slipped from him when slender hands ran up his back. Peace settled over him and his mind calmed. He knew it was Aikaterina doing her magic again. He straightened and turned.

She didn't say anything. She didn't need to. Her touch was a language that spoke to him... to his body. He threaded his fingers through her wet hair and pulled her against him, capturing her lips in a deep kiss. Breaking their kiss, he rested his forehead against hers.

"I like the way you make me... feel," she said.

Bear bit back a low chuckle. She was driving him crazy with the way she was running her hands over his body. A strangled groan slipped from him when her hands dipped lower.

"I like the way you make me feel, too," he confessed, capturing her lips again.

It was late morning by the time they emerged from the bedroom. A part of Bear was glad that it was Christmas Eve, though no one would know it from looking around his cabin. There was no holly. Nor was there a Christmas tree with sparkling lights and candles in the windows. There was no jolly music filling the air.

It would be just like every other day if not for Aikaterina's presence, he dismally thought.

"I need to do my rounds. Unfortunately, ranch life knows no holidays," he said as he placed a plate of eggs and toast in front of her. He looked at the meager meal. "If you want to ride with me, we could go into town for something a little more filling. I didn't buy a lot. Ann Marie usually prepares meals and has Mason deliver them to the few ranch hands who stick around."

"I would enjoy going with you," she replied.

"Sounds good," he said, sitting down across from her to eat his breakfast.

"Tell me of your holiday," she requested.

He looked up from his plate with a surprised expression before he frowned and thought about it. He looked out at the window. It was still snowing—big, beautiful flakes fluttered to the ground. It wasn't heavy as it had been yesterday and last night. No... this was a magical, postcard snow that coated everything in white.

"It is Christmas... for me anyway. Others celebrate Hanukkah or Kwanzaa. For some it is a spiritual time. For others it is a celebration of their culture. I grew up believing it was some fat guy flying around in a sleigh and doing minor breaking-and-entering to drop off gifts in exchange for milk and cookies. My grandmother, Agatha, was a bit unorthodox in her beliefs. She left fine cigars and aged whiskey for the old man," he said with a low chuckle and a shake of his head.

"She was not concerned this man might harm you?" Aikaterina asked.

He laughed again and shook his head. "No. Hell, anyone with any sense knew to steer clear of Agatha. My grandmother is half Northern Arapaho/half Shoshone. Gagu, grandmother, always preferred to be called by her first name. She said calling her Gagu made her feel old. Aggie had made a bit of a name for herself long before I appeared. Anyway, my Christmas consisted of trying to trap the old bastard before he could take off with her cigar and whiskey, but I also wanted to see what he looked like. All I had to go by was what was on the television and Christmas cards. I'd listen for the reindeer when I was little. Once I was old enough to realize that it was all a hoax, Aggie gave up on trying to be the good grandmother, packed up all the Christmas goodies, and we'd sit in front of the fire and each have a cigar and a fine glass of whiskey together."

"She is alive, your Agatha?"

He nodded. "Yeah. She'll probably live as long as you... just joking. She had my mom at a young age and my mom had me at a young age so let's just say Aggie has a few more years to go before she's ready to settle down. She ended up marrying a wealthy old businessman on one of her Vegas trips who left her very well off. She is putting his money to good use supporting the economy."

"This bothers you?"

He shook his head. "Nah, not anymore. It did when I was younger. Now, I tell her to go have fun. It isn't like I need a babysitter anymore," he replied, his voice dropping a notch as memories of his childhood swelled inside him.

You enjoyed your childhood.

He looked across at her and gave her a rueful smile. "Yeah, I did. Once I started working here, Mason and Ann Marie pretty much took me under their wings. Before that, as long as I didn't break any laws—or at least get caught breaking them—and did my chores, Aggie let me run free."

"And there was only one girl that you wanted to spend your life with," she added.

"Yeah… and you can see how that turned out," he said.

He breathed deeply and pushed his chair back. Standing, he gathered their empty plates, took them over to the sink and rinsed them, then placed them in the dishwasher. She rose from her seat and stood watching him in silence.

"You'll need to wear something warm. It'll be freezing, even with the heated seat on the snowmobile," he warned.

She glanced out the window. "The weather does not affect me the way it does humans." She looked back at him. "But, to keep up appearances should we meet others, I will dress appropriately."

He knew his mouth was hanging open when her outfit changed from a pair of white pants and matching silk shirt to blue jeans, a thick, dark-grey turtleneck sweater, and a long fleece-lined wool coat that went down past her calves. Her feet were snug in a pair of dark brown winter boots. On her head, she wore a wide-rim cowboy hat.

"Will this do?" she asked.

He swallowed and nodded. "Yeah. Don't forget a pair of gloves," he reminded her in a hoarse voice.

A pair of gloves appeared in her hand. "Do you need help keeping warm?" she asked.

The teasing light in her eyes told him that she meant the innuendo to help lighten the mood. He walked over to her and wrapped his arms around her. She leaned into him and her soothing calm enfolded him in her warmth.

"You warm me in a way you'll never know," he murmured, leaning down to kiss her.

"Show me your world through your eyes, Bear," she requested.

CHAPTER EIGHT

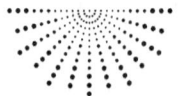

 aldier:

Morah and Hope raced through the access tunnels that connected the different sections of the theme park under the palace. They flashed by Pearl who gave them a thumbs up. The tiger cub took off down a different corridor.

"James, are you sure that Leo can handle the AI duplicator?" Morah breathed into the mic attached to one slender ear.

"I showed him a half dozen times. He promised he could do it," James responded.

"That doesn't mean he can. I'm on my way. Tell him to get over to the graveyard," she instructed.

"Aw, Morah. You know that Leo doesn't like the graveyard. Let him go to the Ghost of Christmas Past. He likes the food and dancing part," James advised.

"Pearl was going there. Sacha is supposed to meet him at the graveyard so they look like Alice and Bálint are walking together," Morah snapped.

"I'll catch up with Sacha and Morah, then we'll go to Christmas Future. Tell James to meet up with Pearl and go to Christmas Present. You meet up with Leo and you two pretend to be Zohar and Roam," Hope said, shifting into a tiny green dragon.

"Tells Leo to meet me at Christmas Past, Sacha goes to Christmas Future, and you and Pearl goes to Christmas Present. Hope is going to meets up with Sacha," Morah relayed with a groan, watching Hope disappear down another tunnel.

"Okay. The parents are splitting ups. You'd better hurry. I heard Auntie Tina say she wanted to make sure Leo wasn't getting into trouble. You're gonna have to make sure he doesn't turn off the AI duplicator where she can see him. Auntie Riley is going with her," James warned.

"Okay, I'll tells him to be careful," Morah replied.

She shifted into her dragon and turned invisible a second before she exited the underground access tunnel. Her eyes widened with alarm and she skidded to a stop seconds before she would have collided with her mom and dad.

Twisting to the side, she crawled under a display table filled with cupcakes and candy treats and waited until they walked by. She shifted back into her two-legged form and peered out from between a gap in the cloth covering.

"It's good to see the kids having so much fun. Cara and Dulce always do an incredible job transforming this place," her dad was saying.

"They do. Trelon was telling me they are working on a new idea for Valentine's Day," her mom replied.

Morah breathed a sigh of relief when they moved away. She was about to crawl out from under the table when she felt a hand grab her back leg. She released a startled yelp and banged her head against the underside of the table. Whipping around, she glared at Leo when he rolled with laughter.

"Leo! You're supposed to be pretending to be Roam," she scolded.

"I am, or I was until I saw you," he replied with a green-tooth grin.

Leo shoved the rest of the bright green cupcake he was holding into his mouth. Her scowl deepened when he licked frosting off his fingers. The AI duplicator would be all sticky if he used it now!

"How did you find me?" she demanded.

Leo tapped his nose, leaving a dot of frosting on the side. "I smelled you. You smell like flowers," he replied with a wiggle of his nose. "I've got a really good sniffer."

Morah snorted and peered out. "Whatever. We've got to go pretend to be Zohar and Roam. Oh, and you've got to be you as well. Your mom is looking for you. We'll meet up with them first so they cans see you and me together, then we need to use the duplicator. You'd better give it to me. You'll make it all sticky if you don't wash your hands first."

Leo snorted. "You sure are bossy. See, they's clean," he grumbled, licking his fingers before holding them up.

Morah shook her head. "That doesn't count. You've gots to *wash* them using water! Now, come on. We've gots to go find your mom," she ordered.

Morah crawled out from under the table and stood up. She growled with impatience and pulled Leo away from the table when he started to reach for another cupcake. Leo grumbled and groaned before grabbing a sucker and following her.

It hard work being in charge! her dragon grumbled as she pulled Leo behind her.

Cat shifters! I'm gonna roast his tail if Leo gets us all in troubles again, she agreed.

∾

Paul Grove's Ranch: Earth

Aikaterina held onto Bear as he navigated the wintry terrain. There was a break in the weather and the snow had stopped. The sun peeked out between heavy gray clouds that promised more snow was on the way.

The weather wouldn't be an issue. If necessary, she could keep the snow from falling until after they returned home later. In the meantime, she did what she could to protect Bear from the freezing temperatures. She had enveloped the snowmobile in a bubble of warmth after he had helped her onto the vehicle.

"Where are we going now?" she asked.

Bear turned his head slightly. "Mason asked me to check on a sleigh that we have. Ann Marie's family wants to go on a Christmas Eve sleigh ride. We have a couple of draft horses we use to pull it. I need to plow the road and check on the sleigh and the other equipment he'll need first, though," he said.

"That sounds like fun."

Bear laughed. "It would be if it was anyone other than Ann Marie's family. Mason swears she was adopted. I think he is right. She's nothing like her siblings or folks."

Bear steered the snowmobile to a large outer building. Aikaterina waited as he pulled under a section that had a roof but no sides to it. He turned off the snowmobile and dismounted before turning to help her off.

"I need to attach the snowplow to the UTV. Since I'm not doing all the roads, and I suspect the family will get bored with the horse and sleigh show once they realize how cold it is, I'm only going to do a short section," he said.

"It sounds exciting," she murmured.

He paused, stared at her for a moment, before they both burst out laughing. He motioned for her to follow him into the barn. She stood to the side and watched him as he connected the snowplow to the front of the UTV. He opened the passenger door for her.

"This is a bit more comfortable and you won't have to do any of your magic to keep me warm. This does have a nice heater in it," he commented.

"I enjoy using my... magic to keep you warm," she replied.

"You can do that later tonight," he said.

He caught her hand before she entered the UTV and kissed her. Pleasure surged through her as did the energy that was slowly fading from her. She turned into his arms and wound her arms around his neck, returning his heated kiss like he had shown her last night.

She blinked when he suddenly released her and turned toward the door. Three men and a woman entered the barn. They all stopped when they caught sight of Bear and her.

"Bear, I thought I heard the snowmobile," Mason said in a loud voice.

"Hey, Mason. I was just getting ready to do some snowplowing," Bear greeted.

"Who's your friend?"

"Merry Christmas, Wayne. This is a friend of mine, Aikaterina," Bear reluctantly introduced.

"We'd better let you get back to what you were doing. Wayne, Al, Mary Beth, and Franklin wanted to go for a walk," Mason explained.

"We don't need to go too quickly," Wayne protested. "How long are you staying, Aikaterina?"

"I haven't decided yet," she responded.

Bear slid his arm around her waist and tried to steer her back to the UTV. She looked at the woman who was two years younger than Bear. Mary Beth's thoughts were very loud... and rude.

Mary Beth has desire for you. She is not happy with me being here.

Bear started and looked over his shoulder at Mary Beth before he returned his attention to her. She continued to study the human woman, curious about the passionate feelings the woman was projecting despite the fact that Bear had never given the woman any encouragement. In fact, he had given Mary Beth the opposite.

"Ann Marie didn't say nothing about you having a… woman friend visiting, Bear," Mary Beth said.

Bear kept his expression neutral as he shut the door to the UTV. *Maybe because it is nobody's business,* he thought.

Aikaterina smiled. *Woman friend is not the word she was thinking. What is a ho—?*

Okay, I think it is time to go, he replied before she completed her thought.

"Yeah, well, that's the beauty of living on my own, I don't have to tell anyone else when I have company coming. I'll get the road cleared. What time do you want to go on the sleigh ride?" he asked, directing his question to Mason.

"After dinner. Ann Marie plans to have it early. Why don't you pick up a couple of plates before you head back down to your cabin? I'll take care of the horses after the ride," Mason said.

"Why don't Bear and his lady friend come to dinner and go on the ride with us?" Wayne suggested.

"I think that would be a wonderful idea," Mary Beth seconded.

"You could use some help with the horses and sleigh, Mason. Your back has been giving you fits with this cold weather," Franklin said.

"It's not that bad," Mason protested.

"That's not what Papa was saying earlier. I heard him say you could barely get in and out of a chair anymore. Poor Ann Marie is having to do more and more between the ranch and caring for you," Al muttered.

"I don't mind taking care of the sleigh and horses afterward, Mason. You've got company," Bear said.

"Then it's settled, Bear... and his friend... will come to dinner tonight and stay for the sleigh ride afterwards," Mary Beth said.

She plans to seduce you away from me.

Bear covered his growl of revulsion behind a cough. "I'll see you later."

Aikaterina laughed when he jerked open the door to the UTV and practically fell into the seat in his haste to get away from the group. Bear started the UTV and drove out the door. Mary Beth's nasty thoughts pierced Aikaterina as they passed.

A strange emotion swept through her. The thought of Bear kissing and holding that woman... bothered her. The fact that he found the woman repulsive didn't seem to matter. Looking in the side mirror, she lifted her hand as the woman stepped out of the barn. A two-foot section of snow on the roof of the barn slid off and landed on the woman's head, dousing her in the frigid fluff. A smile of satisfaction lifted her lips at the woman's startled scream.

"Do I even want to ask?" Bear inquired.

"It might be best if you don't," she replied.

Bear's deep laughter filled the interior of the UTV. She laughed with him, suddenly feeling younger and more vibrant than she had in... *forever...*

A little before four that afternoon, Bear pulled the UTV back into the barn. As much as he hated what was about to happen, he knew that if he didn't show up for dinner that Mason and Ann Marie would never hear the end of how rude their help was and that it was all Mason's fault. He looked at Aikaterina when she placed her hand on his arm.

"It will be fine," she promised.

He shook his head. "I wouldn't wish this family on my worst enemy," he half-heartedly joked.

"I can always—"

He shook his head again when she wiggled her fingers. "Hopefully that won't be necessary. Just... stick close to me. I don't think decking one of Ann Marie's obnoxious brothers, or throttling one or more of her nephews, or telling her vampire of a niece exactly what I think of her, will help the Christmas festivities."

She leaned up and kissed him. "I will be there for you always, Bear," she promised.

He kissed her hard one more time before he pushed open the door and slid out. He walked around the cab of the UTV, opened her door for her, and held out his hand. She gently squeezed his hand and he wondered if she was reading his mind again. If she was, she would see the chaos churning inside him.

They walked across to Mason and Ann Marie's house. Even though it was still light outside, it looked like every light in the house was on. He grimaced when he heard the loud voices, the thunder of feet, and squeals from the younger kids. Everything inside him wanted to turn tail and run.

"You know what... to hell—"

"Bear! Aikaterina! I thought you were going to chicken out," Wayne said in an overloud voice that made Bear's head hurt.

"Hey, Wayne," Bear greeted.

"Well, ain't you prettier than earlier," Wayne commented, holding his hand out to help Aikaterina up the steps.

"Your compliment is unnecessary. I am pleased to meet the people who matter to Paul, Trisha, and Bear," Aikaterina said.

Bear held his breath as she floated up the steps. Fortunately for him, Wayne was too mesmerized by Aikaterina's face to notice that her feet never touched the steps. He looked down and noticed that Mason had installed heated mats to keep the steps from freezing over.

He probably should have waited until after the holidays, he thought, catching the back door a split second before Wayne closed it as if he wasn't there.

"You know Paul and Trisha? There is talk that someone may have murdered the two of them 'cause no one's seen them in years," Wayne said.

"Paul and Trisha are very happy," Aikaterina replied.

"You really do know them?" Wayne asked with surprise.

"Yes."

"Hey, Wayne, Gramps needs help going to the bathroom," Mary Beth yelled.

Wayne grimaced. "Sorry about that. I'll be right back," he mumbled.

"Thank you, Gramps! Here, let me take your coat," Bear murmured.

She smiled at him and unzipped her coat. Bear slid his hands over her shoulders, giving them a slight squeeze in gratitude for her patience. She slightly turned and pressed a light kiss to his lips.

"Bear, I'm so glad you could make it. Why don't you two go in and rescue Mason from my nieces and nephews. They are hyped up on candy canes," Ann Marie called as she whizzed by them.

"I will help you with the table," Aikaterina stated.

It was impossible to miss the lines of stress around Ann Marie's mouth or the harried expression on her face. From the looks of it, everyone had abandoned the kitchen duties and expected to be catered to. Anger flared inside Bear. Ann Marie must have noticed because she stopped and placed her hand on his arm.

"I'm okay. It's Mason I'm worried about. He has been helping me when he isn't being commanded to fix something that one of the kids have broken. I swear this is the last time they will come here," Ann Marie vowed, her gaze locking on Aikaterina. "I want to apologize."

"For what?" Aikaterina asked with a puzzle frown.

"For humanity. Please do not judge the rest of the humans by my family," Ann Marie replied with a tired grin.

Aikaterina laughed and shook her head. "I have met many species during my existence. I can assure you that your family cannot be as bad as some."

"Well, don't say I didn't warn you," Ann Marie said with a chuckle.

"What do you need to do?" Aikaterina asked.

"Set the table and help place the food on it," Ann Marie said. "Bear, maybe you can carve the turkey before you go rescue my husband."

"It is done," Aikaterina replied with a serene smile.

"Done?" Ann Marie repeated, looking toward the empty dining room.

"Aikaterina," Bear cautioned, glancing through the other door that led into the living room.

"No one noticed. They are too concerned with their own desires," she replied.

Ann Marie looked back and forth from the elaborately set dining room table filled with the food she had been slaving away cooking all day to Aikaterina and back again. Aikaterina reached out and steadied Ann Marie when she swayed on her feet. Bear moved around to Ann Marie's other side.

"Praise be, thank you, Aikaterina," Ann Marie breathed out. Ann Marie turned to look at Bear with a fierce expression. "You need to keep this one."

He laughed and looked over Ann Marie's head at Aikaterina. She returned his smile. His smile faltered and faded as they stood staring at each other. Memories of seeing her standing in the forest, the curiosity in her eyes as she tasted hot chocolate for the first time, their first kiss... their night together—everything around him blurred until he felt like it was just the two of them in the universe.

"Bear... Bear...," Ann Marie was saying.

He blinked and stared down blankly at Ann Marie. "I'm sorry. What did you need?"

Ann Marie patted his arm. "You two go find a seat before I call the others in. Once they know food is on the table, it will be World War III."

CHAPTER NINE

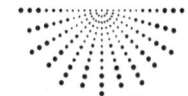

"*W*hy do we have to decorate Bear's house again?" Roam asked, tugging on the tree that he and Bálint had cut down.

"Because it's Christmas and we are going to be the ghosts of Christmas and it is kind-of hard to do if it doesn't even *look* like Christmas," Spring retorted.

"Put the tree in front of the window," Alice instructed.

"Who put you in charge?" Roam growled.

Zohar vigorously shook his head at Roam. "Roam, why don't you go help Jabir with his beasts?" he suggested.

Roam's eyes widened and he nodded. "That sounds like a lot more fun than decorating," he said.

Spring stood aside but growled under her breath at Roam as he charged out of the cabin. Phoenix walked over and gave her sister a hug. Spring sighed and shook her head.

"I'm not sure he is ever going to get any better," Spring muttered.

"If he was like the other boys, he'd drive you even crazier," Phoenix teased.

Spring gave her a grudging smile and sighed again. "You're probably right."

"Bálint, push it to your right. No, your other right," Alice ordered.

"Amber, Jade, and I have the outside ready. You are going to love it!" Adaline exclaimed with excitement.

"You girls don't think there being a Christmas tree on the inside is going to give away what we are doing, do you?" Zohar asked.

Phoenix looked over and giggled. Zohar was almost buried behind the six-foot tall tree. She shook her head.

"I don't think so. He'll think Santa brought it," she answered with a confident expression.

"I can't believe that Santa has been able to make it all the way to our worlds," Adaline said.

Phoenix grinned. "If he can make portal mirrors like me, it's a piece of cake."

"That's perfect. Now, don't move," Alice instructed.

Phoenix and Spring sat down on the couch and watched as Alice created a base for the tree to hold it upright. Once she was done, the boys climbed out from behind the tree. They stood looking at the tree with a frown.

"It doesn't look as fluffy in here as it did outside," Zohar commented.

Bálint shook his head. "It's going to have to do because I'm not cutting another one down."

"Adaline, help me decorate it," Alice said.

"I know, with tiny bears in all different poses," Adaline exclaimed.

"And gold stars… for Aikaterina," Spring added.

"Bálint and I are going to go check on Roam and Jabir. I don't think it is a good idea to leave those two alone for very long," Zohar said.

"That's a good idea. We'll meet you back at the bunkhouse. Remember, we have to be home for Christmas Eve dinner then get back here," Phoenix cautioned.

"I'll remember," Zohar promised.

~

"It's too cold for me," Al grumbled.

"I'm hungry," Jim Bo groaned.

"This would be better if you had reindeer like Santa," complained Hailey.

"Yeah. That would be way cooler than this; especially if they could fly," Jeff groaned.

"How is this supposed to be fun? I can't see anything and there's no internet connection," Ralphie whined.

Bear gritted his teeth and snapped the reins. The two draft horses turned in a big loop at his command. He had taken over driving the sleigh from Mason. Wayne sat next to him while two of Ann Marie's siblings and four of her nieces and nephews sat in the back. The only one not complaining was Wayne and Bear wasn't making any promises the man would live to make it back to the house.

"So, how long have you and Aikaterina been an item?" Wayne asked.

"Since yesterday," he replied.

Wayne's eyes widened and he stared at Bear in disbelief. "When did you meet her?"

"Yesterday," he answered.

Bear felt like groaning. *I probably shouldn't have answered him but he is annoying the hell out of me.*

I care not what he thinks of me. Ann Marie was right. He is a lowly creature, she responded.

Bear covered his bark of laughter with a cough. "I think we should call it a night. It's getting too dark to see anything and the temperature is dropping. I'm sure everyone will be happier in a warm house," he said.

"And having internet," Ralphie added.

"How serious is it between you two?" Wayne persisted.

"That's none of your damn business, Wayne," Bear growled.

"I'm just testing the possibilities, Bear. No sense in taking offense, man," Wayne complained.

"You are being rude," Bear snapped.

"Maybe. Personally, I think you're unsure of your little friend's affection," Wayne retorted.

"Wayne, why don't you sit back here and let me sit upfront with Bear on the way back," Mary Beth sweetly suggested.

Bear gritted his teeth. Between having a choice between Wayne and Mary Beth, he didn't know which was worse. Aikaterina's lilting laughter echoed in his head.

Coward! he teased.

Ann Marie needed help with cleaning up. No one else volunteered, she sweetly replied.

I'm sure you did it in record time, he retorted with amusement.

Of course! I've never washed a dish in my life. I wasn't about to tell poor Ann Marie that!

His laughter was cut short when Mary Beth slid her hand up along his thigh. While he had been having his silent conversation with Aikaterina, Mary Beth and Wayne had traded places. He was about to say something when a large pile of snow fell from a tree as they passed under it and landed on top of Mary Beth, dousing her once again in a pile of frigid fluff as she squealed like a pig.

Thank you!

Her laughter was the only response he needed to know that the sudden snow fall was no accident.

Aikaterina hugged Ann Marie, giving her new friend a boost of energy. She did the same to Mason before Bear led her back to the barn to get the snowmobile. They were halfway across the yard when a sudden wave of fatigue struck her.

Bear's startled hiss of dismay made her realize that the arm he had around her, passed through her. She desperately pulled at the energy surrounding them, seeking to re-establish her form. Bear stood in front of her, his eyes filled with concern.

"Are you alright?" he asked.

She nodded. "Yes, I'm fine. It was a mere slip," she assured him.

He tentatively touched her to make sure his fingers didn't pass through her. His grip tightened around her when he realized that she was in her solid corporeal form. He quickly guided her to the snowmobile.

She held onto him all the way back. For once, the chill in the air seemed to seep into her. She was too weak to pull together enough energy to wrap them in a warm cocoon. It was taking everything in her power to keep her form from fading.

Bear must have sensed her weakness because he pushed the snowmobile to the max. They slid around the curve of the road. The trip back seemed to take forever. Bear placed his hand over hers for a moment when they hit a straight, relatively flat section of the road. He was forced to release her when they crested a hill and traveled along a series of curves.

A half hour later, his cabin came into view. The snowmobile slid the last few feet under the lean-to and he turned it off. He dismounted the bike, all the while keeping one hand on her. He gently scooped her up into his arms and carried her toward his cabin.

"Tell me what's wrong," he demanded, climbing the steps.

"I… am… fading," she murmured, turning her face into him.

"Fading? What the hell does fading mean?"

He silently cursed as he fumbled with the door. Breathing heavily, he pushed the door open with his foot and stepped inside. He didn't bother with any of the lights. Instead, he strode through into the living room.

"Love, tell me what I need to do," he said, gently lowering her to the couch.

She lifted her hand to caress his face. "I only need a little time to… rest," she murmured, closing her eyes.

She was fading and this time there was nothing she could do to stop her body from turning to mist. That form required less energy. Bear staggered back from the couch, sinking down into the chair he had sat in earlier. She reached out to touch him, but her hand brushed through his flesh.

Oh, my beautiful human, she mourned.

Distraught that she might never touch him again, she floated over to kneel beside him. If she had a heart, it would be breaking at that moment. Unable to bear the look of sorrow and despair on his face, she flowed out of the cabin and into the cold outside. In her grief, she continued to the edge of the woods.

She stopped and looked up at the stars. Instead of the peace she thought might come knowing she would become one with them again, she wanted to cry out against the ache building inside her.

I've had the power to create galaxies; and yet, I have never truly known what it means to experience love and life until now. How do the other species cope with such grief? she wondered as shimmering gold tears dripped into the pristine white snow under her.

Bear sat in his darkened living room in numb shock. One moment, Aikaterina had been lying on the couch, the next she was gone. He briefly thought he had felt her touch. That changed when the chilled air of the cabin settled over him.

I should never have opened my heart again, he thought as the pain inside him grew.

"I should never have opened my heart again," he repeated with growing anger, rising from the chair, and walking over to the fireplace.

He braced his hands against the mantle and stared into the glowing embers. Closing his eyes, he breathed deeply, trying to push the sense of despair away. How could he feel so deeply after just one night with her? How was it possible that he was...?

"No, damn it! No, I wasn't falling in love," he swore, opening his eyes and staring at the picture of Samara and Adaline.

Tears burned the back of his eyes and his throat closed up as they stared back at him. Was he destined to spend his life alone? He reached up and ran his finger down along the frame.

"Hi, Bear."

He stiffened, staring at the picture in shock when he heard the lilting voice of Adaline. He shook his head, wondering if he was going crazy. The sudden reflection of Christmas lights in the glass made him blink. He slowly turned until he was facing in the direction the voice had come from... and blinked again.

"Adaline?" he choked out, staring at the slender girl standing in front of a brightly decorated Christmas tree.

How the hell did I miss this? he wondered.

"I missed you!" Adaline said.

He opened his arms and caught her when she surged forward. Winding his arms around her, he lowered his head and breathed in her fresh, earthly scent. She held onto him tightly, hugging him back as she used to.

"You've grown," he whispered, noticing how tall she was getting.

"That happens," she laughed.

He pulled back and stared down at her in wonder. Tears dampened her flushed cheeks. Her eyes were bright and filled with warmth, making him almost believe that she was real. He touched her cheek.

"You have your mother's smile," he murmured.

"You haven't changed. Mom and I have missed you," she said.

"Are you real?"

He touched her hair. It felt real. She pinched his side. He started at the unexpected pain.

"Yes. I'm real," she replied with a broad grin.

He shook his head. "How is this possible? Is your mom—" He looked around the room with a frown.

"She's not here," Adaline said.

"How…? What are you doing here?"

She smiled. "I'm your Ghost of Christmas Past. I'm here to help you realize that everything is okay… and, well, also to help Aikaterina," she said.

"How did you know about Aikaterina? Ghost of Christmas Past? Like in a Christmas Carol? Adaline, what is going on?" he demanded, growing more confused by the minute.

"Yes, well, sort of like in a Christmas Carol. You aren't anything like Scrooge, so this is a little different; plus, I need a little more help," she began.

He shook his head, released her, and walked over to sit back down in the chair. He stared at the Christmas tree, trying to understand exactly what was happening. He ran his hand through his hair and down his face.

"Maybe you'd better explain. First, how did you get here? Second, does your mom... and dad know you are here? Third, what do you mean you need a little help?" he asked.

Adaline walked over and scooped his hand up into hers. She held it tightly, biting her lip. His heart tightened as he noticed how much she had grown over the past few years.

"Jade, I'm ready," Adaline called out.

"Who is Jade—?"

The question died on his lips when the walls of his cabin changed. He blinked in shock. Adaline sat down on the arm of the chair and grinned. It was like he was in a three-dimensional, virtual movie. Ghostly images of the past came to life. He recognized the different scenes from videos that Samara had taken over the years.

"That's me when mom came home from the hospital. She was so tired, but you were there. She used to tell me stories about how you would walk me for hours so she could get some rest," she said.

He released a strained chuckle and nodded. "You would snuggle up against my chest and suck on your thumb. Every time I would stop, you would wake up and give me this glare until I started walking again."

The scene changed and he caught his breath. "I remember when your mom first told me about there being aliens on the ranch. I didn't believe her at first, but it didn't take long to convince me."

Adaline giggled when the baby in the crib wiggled her fingers and the cheerful mobile of stuffed giraffes, lions, and stars above the crib began to move and dance. Scene after scene played out. Bear relived the joy and wonder of being a part of Adaline and Samara's lives.

"Mom, what do you want to tell Bear?" Adaline's younger self asked, unsteadily aiming the phone camera at her mom.

Bear smiled. Samara was in the middle of brushing down a horse. He recognized the barn from the horse farm that Samara had moved to. A bittersweet emotion swept through him when Samara paused and looked at the camera.

"Hi, Bear. I hope you are doing well and happy. Adaline and I miss you. You'd be proud of Adaline. She has your touch when it comes to training horses."

Adaline's face suddenly appeared, taking up the entire screen. He was looking up her nose. She grinned at him.

"I miss you more. Mom is still single, by the way. Maybe you can come out here and visit us," the young Adaline said.

Bear swallowed. The more he studied Samara, the more he realized that he hadn't felt the same excruciating pain when they had left that he was experiencing now. He had felt lonely and he had missed Samara, but mostly he missed Adaline.

He sat forward when the scenes changed to a different world. Alien structures, flora, and fauna held him captivated as he studied the changing images.

"That's Ceran-Pax, the Curizan home world. We live in a really cool house on the palace grounds, but we also spend a lot of time on Valdier. Sometimes we visit other worlds or space stations," Adaline explained.

"Who... or what... is that?" he asked.

Adaline appeared to be playing with a group of children. Some of them looked human... or at least humanish. Others were definitely alien. There were four lizard-like creatures with two heads each playing with two green blobs that looked almost like Jell-O. Mixed in with them were other kids who changed into dragons. It was obvious they were children from the way they were racing around the playground.

"Those are Uncle Fred and Uncle Bob's kids. The two-headed lizard kids are called Tiliqua. They are real smart, especially with numbers. The green, Jell-O-ones are called Gelation. They are super fun to play Red Rover with. I taught everyone that game. Rudd and Pi can change into all kinds of weird shapes. You don't want to play catch with them, though. If the ball gets inside them, it is super yucky afterwards." She said with a laugh. "That's Alice. She's my cousin. The dragons are from Valdier and the tiger-shifters are called Sarafin. Roam and Leo are always getting into trouble. There are also Sacha and Pearl, but they weren't with us that day."

"What about your mom?" he curiously asked.

The scene changed to Samara and Adalard. He sat back and studied both of their expressions. It was impossible to miss the love between them. Samara glowed with happiness. He swallowed when he saw the protective way Adalard stayed close to Samara.

"Adalard!"

Samara squealed when Adalard came up behind her, wrapped his arms around her, and playfully lifted her off her feet. Samara's face flushed and she leaned her head back to kiss Adalard. Several women laughed at the display.

"Those are my Aunties. They aren't really my *real* aunts, but they are part of our family," Adaline explained.

He recognized Trisha Grove and Ariel and Carmen from high school. He took a deep breath when he noticed Paul Grove standing in the background with his arm around an exquisite woman. He was holding a dark-haired little girl in his arms.

"That's Grandpa Paul and Grandma Morian and Morah. Morah is bossy, but I like her," Adaline explained.

As the scenes faded, he was left staring at the Christmas tree that hadn't been there earlier. His chest felt tight as emotion swept through him. He pulled his gaze away from the tree to look at Adaline.

"We have so many great memories with you. Mom said that is a gift that can never be taken away from us," she said.

"You never told me how you came here... or why," he murmured.

Adaline smiled. "Christmas magic. We came here because we want you to be happy and not feel lonely anymore. You have a really good heart. We think you can save Aikaterina."

He sat forward and studied Adaline's face. "What do you mean... save Aikaterina? How?"

His voice was edged with urgency. He didn't know how a bunch of kids would know what to do, but he was willing to try anything... everything... if there was a chance it might bring Aikaterina back to him.

Hell, if there really was such a thing as Christmas magic, he would get down on his knees and pray to whatever Santa was out there.

"You have to believe. Her colors get stronger when you are with her. Believe in her and love her—like you did mom and me," Adaline said, kneeling in front of him and grasping his hands. "It helped my mom, and Phoenix and Alice said it saved their moms, too. If you love her, you can make her better."

"I don't think that is how things work, Adaline," he gently replied.

Adaline squeezed his hands and gave him a pleading look. "You've got to believe, Bear. We really think this will work. You just have to believe in the magic. Aikaterina glows when she is with you," Adaline said, her voice laced with hope.

CHAPTER TEN

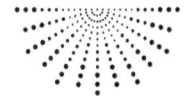

"*A*ikaterina."

Aikaterina focused on the soft voice pulling at her. Her essence was very weak and it took everything inside her to follow the thread. A soothing hand brushed against her and she thought for a moment that Arilla or Arosa had come for her.

Perhaps their energy could help me return to the Hive.

That thought faded when the essence of a very young and powerful girl wrapped around her. Aikaterina would have smiled if she was in a form to do so. She recognized Phoenix Reykill's unusual energy.

Phoenix's power had called to her the moment she was conceived. On very, very, very rare occasions, a being was destined to be born who would change the course of many worlds within the multiverse. Phoenix was such a soul. Her powers were still being defined and developed, but her pure heart assured that she would be a force of good to many, many worlds.

"Oh, little one. You should be home with your family," she murmured, connecting with Phoenix's energy.

"I am with family. You are a part of our family, Aikaterina. The other dragonlings and I love you so much," Phoenix said.

Aikaterina gently stroked the colorful bands weaving to hold her to this world. Phoenix had an old soul, one that would rival her own. She wanted to pull away so that Phoenix wouldn't experience the emptiness that was sure to follow her passing, but the young girl refused to release her.

"I will miss the many adventures of all you dragonlings and your friends," she mourned.

Phoenix's energy surged through her. Aikaterina absorbed the flow, forming into a translucent version of her corporeal form. Phoenix stepped closer and smiled.

"You don't have to. It's not your time to fade," Phoenix insisted.

Aikaterina shook her head. "Your essence is the only thing keeping me here, child. I have lived a very long time. Even a Goddess should not live forever."

"But… you are more than a Goddess to us. You are part of our family and we don't give up on family," Phoenix insisted, reaching out to grasp her hand.

Aikaterina looked at their entwined hands. Phoenix's hand should have passed through hers. While she had the illusion of a corporeal form, she was still made of mist. Yet, she could feel the young girl's warmth and the strength of her grip.

"You have such a kind heart. The universe chose well when it saw you," Aikaterina murmured.

Phoenix stepped closer and wrapped her arms around Aikaterina, hugging her as if she would never let her go. Aikaterina bowed her head and held onto the fragile body. How could so much love and compassion be contained in such a small form?

Aikaterina frowned when she felt a strange flutter deep inside her. Her form grew stronger as Phoenix opened her heart and mind. Aikaterina saw visions of the times she had visited with the young girl.

I enjoyed watching you and the others hunt for the colorful eggs, she mused, remembering the first time the dragon-shifting men and their families experienced an Earth holiday.

You helped me save momma.

You did that on your own, child. Your love for her opened the doorway, which helped to give her the time she needed and a dream to hold onto—even if she wasn't ready to accept it, she replied.

You guided our parents and helped protect them when they were in danger, Phoenix insisted.

I merely showed them the power they had within them.

You have that power still inside you. We are not the only ones that need you. Bear needs you, too.

Aikaterina closed her eyes and tilted her head back as visions of Bear swept through her. Warmth surged through her and she knew if she opened her eyes, she would see her body shimmering with power. The flutter in her chest grew and she fought to hold onto it. Confusion filled her when the visions changed.

The universe isn't ready for you to fade. It is ready for you to evolve.

Aikaterina stared around her in wonder. Her lips parted when she saw Bear standing a short distance away from her. He was watching her with an intense expression. His eyes were warm and determined.

"Bear," she said, lifting her hand in his direction.

Phoenix released her and stepped back. "Your future is not only on Valdier, but here. Your destiny is not to observe life, but to experience it. It is the only way any species can grow and understand. Love gives you the strength to find your way back. This can be your future if you believe."

Aikaterina gazed longingly at Bear. She wanted to believe that he could love her. She thought of Arosa and her love for Tamblin, and hope filled her. Was it possible for an ancient to love a human?

Anything is possible if you believe.

Aikaterina turned when she heard the melody of music rising around her. All around her brilliant, colorful lights flickered to life. Her lips parted and a smile of awe curved her lips. It was as if the dragonlings had captured the magic of the universe and decorated the forest with it. Their energy fed her, giving her renewed strength.

Garlands and colorful decorations hung from the branches of the trees and lit up the lower shrubs. The lights danced across the brilliant white snow. Around her, the children stepped closer, forming a circle until they could grasp each other's hands.

Animals, large and small, gathered behind them. Aikaterina bowed her head to the buck when he lowered his head to her. The flutter in her chest grew so strong that she placed her hand against it, afraid that it would burst out.

She looked down at her hand, turning it back and forth when she noticed that she had returned to her corporeal form. Her lips parted with surprise and she looked up at Phoenix. Standing on each side of Phoenix, she saw Arilla and Arosa. As she turned to look at the other children, she noticed more of her kind appearing.

"Aikaterina."

She slowly turned when she heard the low, urgent male voice call her name. Her eyes locked with Bear's. He stood in a gap that formed to open for him. She gave him a soothing smile when he took a step forward then paused.

"Bear," she called, holding out her hand to him.

He slowly walked toward her and took her hand. He looked down at their entwined fingers and she gently squeezed them. She pulled him closer to her when he looked back up.

"Do you believe in the magic of Christmas?" she asked.

He released a strained laugh before he lifted his hand to cup her cheek. "I do now."

She leaned into him, capturing his lips. He pulled her closer and she wound her arms around his neck. As the first flakes of snow began to fall at the stroke of midnight, she envisioned them back in the cabin. Her eyes opened wide when nothing happened.

He looked down at her and smiled. "Let's go home," he said, wrapping his arm around her waist.

"I would like that," she said.

He paused and looked around them with a frown. "Where did everyone go?"

She laughed and looked up at the stars. "Home. It is Christmas after all."

"What do you mean 'You lost them?'" Spring demanded, staring with disbelief at Jabir.

Jabir lifted his shoulders and raised his hands up. "They were there one second and the next they were gone, isn't that right, Roam?"

"Yep, just like Alice and Adaline, only they just went—" Roam said finishing his sentence with a whistle and a lift of his hand into the air.

"What is that supposed to mean?" Spring growled.

"It means they flew away," Zohar clarified.

"Oh, man! That is so cool. Flying Poro!" Jade and Amber crowed with glee.

Phoenix groaned along with her sister. "We've got to find them," she said.

"How? They could be anywhere," Alice replied, glaring at Jabir.

"Maybe Bálint could track them," Roam suggested.

"Uh, I can track things on the ground. If they are flying, they aren't going to leave any tracks," Bálint pointed out.

"Unless they poop while they're flying," Amber pointed out.

Bálint nodded. "That's true."

"Or we could use the tracking device in their harnesses. Asim and Dad make sure all our animals have tracking devices in case they get out," Jabir said.

"Why didn't you tell us that in the first place?" Spring growled.

Jabir shrugged. "'Cause I just remembered it," he responded with a lopsided grin.

"Amber, do you and Jade have anything that can track them?" Phoenix asked.

Phoenix watched as the two sisters put their heads together and frantically whispered back and forth before they looked up and nodded.

"Yep. We just need the frequencies," Amber said.

"Jabir, you help Amber and Jade. Bálint, you check if the Poro left a poop trail. Spring, you, me, and Zohar will take to the air and see if we can see them," Phoenix instructed.

"What do you want me to do?" Roam asked.

Spring looked at Roam and raised an eyebrow. "You've got a super sniffer. Go with Bálint and use your nose."

"It can't be any worse than smelling you after you've been digging in the dirt all day," Roam snapped before turning away.

Phoenix caught her sister's arm when she bent to pick up at handful of snow. Spring grinned at her and dropped the snow back to the ground. Phoenix was surprised. She thought Spring would have been upset by Roam's retort.

"He told me he loves the smell of me after playing in the garden all day," Spring confided with a softened gaze in the direction that Roam and Bálint went.

"You two are weird," Phoenix muttered.

"What do you want us to do, Phoenix?" Alice asked.

Phoenix bit her lip and looked at the two Curizan princesses. "Can you two checkout the houses just in case Jabir's beasts went there? Adaline knows her way around better than we do and you both can pop in and out without being seen."

"There are several barns along the way. They may look for a place out of the weather. We'll check them out," Adaline said.

"Let's go."

Phoenix shifted into her dragon and lifted off the ground, followed by Spring and Zohar. Hopefully, it wouldn't be hard to find the beasts. If they didn't find them and their parents found out, they would be in so much trouble!

I wonder if this will put us on Santa's naughty list, Spring wondered.

I hope not. I was really looking forward to opening presents tomorrow, Zohar groaned.

Today. It is already Christmas. Hopefully, Santa already visited the palace before he finds out what happened.

Or maybe he'll need some more reindeer and we can tell him we brought them for him as a present, Spring added.

That good idea.

Phoenix chuckled at her dragon's eager response. She liked that idea, too. Perhaps it was time Santa received a present instead of him giving one.

∽

An hour later, Phoenix, Spring, and Zohar landed back at the bunkhouse. They hadn't had any luck finding the Poro. She looked up when Jade opened the cabin door and shook her head.

"Nothing yet. Jabir wasn't sure what the frequency on the tracking devices are. So far, we've listened to dozens of radio stations, airports, police scanners, and a bunch of guys talking about hams on radios."

"Hey, I think I've got something," Amber called.

Phoenix rushed past Jade into the cabin. "Is it close?"

"Yeah," Amber replied, looking up from the screen she was holding.

They all turned when Alice suddenly appeared in the room behind them. She grinned at them.

"Phoenix, we've found them. Adaline is trying to get them down off the roof," Alice's excited voice exclaimed.

"Off the roof?" Phoenix repeated.

"Yeah. They are at the main house. They were in the barn, but they flew out when we popped inside," Alice explained.

"Where's Jabir? If anyone can help capture them, he can," Zohar said.

"I think we should all go. Phoenix, if you can create a portal, maybe we could ride them through it back to Valdier," Spring suggested.

Phoenix bit her lip and thought about it. She looked at Alice and Zohar. They both nodded.

"I think that is a great idea," Zohar said.

"Okay. Alice, let the others know. We'll fly to the house. Where are Bálint and Roam?"

"They're at the main house," Jade said, looking up and grinning. "We put a tracker on Roam."

"For security purposes," Amber added.

Spring snorted with amusement. "Don't tell him. That might come in handy when we play tag," she said.

Amber and Jade giggled.

"You'd better not put one on me," Zohar growled in warning at the twins.

"Oh, we'd never do that, would we, Jade?" Amber said, looking at her twin with an innocent expression.

"Never," Jade replied with a snicker.

Zohar gave the sisters another glare.

"Let's go."

Amber and Jade nodded and quickly collected their bag of goodies. Minutes later, the small group took to the air. Phoenix breathed a sigh of relief when she saw the eight Poro on the roof of the main house. Jabir was talking to them and the alien reindeer appeared to be listening as he explained their plans.

Phoenix landed next to Jabir as he petted the forehead of the largest Poro. He looked at her with a pleading expression. She frowned and looked from him to the Poro and back again.

"What's wrong?" she asked.

Jabir continued to caress the Poro. "They really miss their home. Pocko wanted me to ask you if you could send them home."

Phoenix frowned and looked at the Poro. "But... I don't know where they live," she said in a hesitant voice.

"Asim said they came from Orbay Twine," Jabir replied.

"Amber and I could look it up on the star charts. We downloaded the entire collection when we were working on the spaceship we were building," Jade said.

Phoenix reached out and stroked Pocko. "If Amber and Jade show me your home, I'll send you there," she promised.

Pocko stomped his front hooves on the roof and bowed his head. Jabir leaned forward and wrapped his arms around the Poro's neck. Phoenix watched with a bemused expression. How Jabir talked to animals always amazed her.

"Uh, Phoenix. There are lights coming on," Roam warned, peering over the edge.

Phoenix groaned and frantically motioned for the others to pick a beast to get on. She lifted an eyebrow when Roam reached down and scooped her sister up, placed her on the back of Pocko, before jumping up behind her. Spring flushed when Roam wrapped his arm around her waist.

Shifting into her dragon, Phoenix flew over the driveway and began forming the portal that would take them all home. As the portal began to form, the bang of the screen door below distracted her and she looked down. Her eyes widened when she saw a group of humans, including children, emerge out onto the snow-covered drive.

"Now," she said, looking over at her friends.

One-by-one, the Poro trotted across the roof before leaping into the air. They moved their legs as if they were running. Phoenix's dragon purred with pleasure. She didn't know if the others could see what she did, but the Poro were running on a stream of energy. The line curved and flowed through the portal. Phoenix counted both Poro and Dragonlings as they passed through to make sure that no one was left behind. Only when the last one disappeared through to Valdier did she sweep through the opening, pulling it closed behind her.

"Did you see that!" Wayne exclaimed in awe.

"It was Santa's reindeer and his elves," Ralphie shouted with excitement.

"I thought he wasn't real," Mary Beth mumbled.

"I told you that you should have been nicer, Mary Beth," Gramps grumbled.

Mary Beth opened her mouth to retort, but her response came out as a squeal as a layer of snow from the roof toppled onto her head.

"Ew, what is that smell?" Hailey muttered, looking at the bits of brown mixed in with the snow.

Ann Marie gently nudged Mason in the side and pointed up at the roof from where the snow had fallen. Above them, they stared in awe at the figures of two golden Goddesses who stared down on them with a mischievous grin before disappearing.

"Maybe there really is a Santa Claus," Mason whispered.

"If there is, that was the best present ever," Ann Marie chuckled. "God, I love this place!" she sighed, leaning back against him.

EPILOGUE

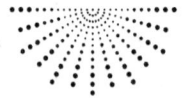

 aldier:

"I can't believe the kids are still asleep! It's Christmas morning!" Trelon muttered.

"They are teenagers," Zoran said, looking up from the report he was reading.

"I would agree with that, but even the younger kids are still in bed," Viper pointed out. "Leo never sleeps this late."

"Neither does Pearl. Sacha... maybe, Pearl... never!" Riley commented, biting her fingernail with worry.

"Mandra, have you seen Jabir's new pets?" Asim asked, striding into the room.

"No, why?" Mandra asked, pausing as he poured himself a cup of coffee.

"Because according to the tracking device, either they sprouted wings and flew home, or there is something wrong with the microchips we embedded under their skin," Asim replied.

Mandra frowned. "What do you mean? They should be at the mountain home," he said.

Asim shook his head. "I'm not talking about the mountain. I'm talking about their home-- Orbay Twine."

Mandra took the scanner from Asim and studied the location with a frown. Trelon, Kelan, and Zoran rose from their seats to look over his shoulder. The same thought hit all the men at the same time and they looked at each other with growing panic.

"The spaceship…." Trelon said.

"You don't think they…." Zoran groaned.

"Anything is possible with Trelon's girls," Kelan added.

Trelon glared at his brother. "Hey, they had some help," he protested.

"I think we'd better check on them," Viper muttered.

Zoran looked toward the doorway and sighed with relief when the squeals of delight and laughter echoed through into the dining area that had been set up. The men walked over to the doorway and peered into the other room. The room was filled with dragonlings, from the youngest to the oldest.

"Here, Phoenix, this is for you," Zohar said.

"Jabir, I got you a present and some for your animal friends," Bálint was saying.

"Jade, look at what Santa brought me!" James exclaimed, holding up a miniature splicer.

"Trelon? Really?" Kelan groaned.

Trelon grinned. "He built his first robot the other day. I think he is going to be just like his sisters."

"Merry Christmas, everyone!" Cara called out.

"Merry Christmas!"

"Zoran, do you know what this is?" Abby asked, holding up a strange-looking device. "I found it in Morah's pocket when I went to wash clothes this morning."

Zoran took the device and pressed the button.

"Oh, dear," Cara muttered, looking at Zoran with wide eyes.

"What's the matter?"

Trelon snorted and slapped his oldest brother on the shoulder. "Not a thing… not a thing."

Zoran frowned and looked at his reflection in the mirror hanging on the far wall. He blinked when the perfect image of Roam stared back at him. Understanding dawned, and he looked up in time to see his son nudge Roam. The kids stared back at them with an apologetic expression.

"Does anyone want to explain this?" Zoran asked, holding up the AI duplicator.

Morah rose to her feet and put her hands on her hips. "Yes. But first let me say, it is a *lot* of work being a dragonling!"

Earth: One month later

Arosa watched Aikaterina and Bear through the mirror Arilla was holding. She worried her lip as she studied the couple. Arilla sighed and lowered the mirror.

"Do you think we did the right thing?" Arilla asked.

"We had no choice. If we hadn't agreed, the council would have destroyed her," Arosa said.

"But, taking her memories," she fretted.

"The Council of Ancients threatened to wipe Bear's lifeline and destroy Aikaterina once and for all. Losing Bear would have done that. Just because the council doesn't believe Aikaterina could ever love a human, doesn't make it so.

"But one human month! That isn't even a blink of an eye."

"It was all they would give us. We had to save Aikaterina and Bear. Bear knows what is at stake. At least they let him keep his memories," Arosa said.

"Yes, but with restrictions," Arilla pointed out, pulling up the mirror again.

Arosa covered her sister's hand and gently took the mirror. "Believe in the magic, sister. Bear will save Aikaterina. He knows what is at stake. Only he has the power to wake the sleeping Goddess inside her."

They both looked down on Aikaterina's sleeping form, hoping that the magic of Christmas worked all year long.

To Be Continued:
WAKING A GOLDEN GODDESS

The Ancients have given Bear Running Wolf one month to save the life of the woman he loves, his own lifeline, and the lives of the Valdier, Sarafin, and Curizan. He will do whatever it takes to prove them wrong and show that humans have a power far greater than any they have seen—the power not only to wake a golden goddess, but to love her.

Note from the Author:

Christmas for a Goddess was an unexpected story. I was not planning on writing this story, but once I started, I couldn't wait to see where it led me. Bear and Aikaterina's story is just beginning. Waking a Golden Goddess is on my list to write this year, so expect more exciting tales from the Dragon Lords of Valdier series!

ADDITIONAL BOOKS

If you loved this story by me (Susan aka S.E. Smith) please leave a review! My websites are https://sesmithfl.com and https://sesmithya.com. Be sure to sign up for my newsletter to hear about new releases. Find your favorite way to keep in touch here: https://sesmithfl.com/contact-me/

RECOMMENDED READING ORDER LISTS:

https://sesmithfl.com/reading-list-by-events/

https://sesmithfl.com/reading-list-by-series/

MY GENRES:

Contemporary / Romance

GIRLS FROM THE STREET

She was born on the streets; he was born to rule.

Science Fiction / Romance

DRAGON LORDS OF VALDIER

It all started with a king who crashed on Earth, desperately hurt. He inadvertently discovered a species that would save his own.

CURIZAN WARRIOR

The Curizans have a secret, kept even from their closest allies, but even they are not immune to the draw of a little known species from an isolated planet called Earth.

MARASTIN DOW WARRIORS

The Marastin Dow are reviled and feared for their ruthlessness, but not all want to live a life of murder. Some wait for just the right time to escape....

SARAFIN WARRIORS

A hilariously ridiculous human family who happen to be quite formidable... and a secret hidden on Earth. The origin of the Sarafin species is more than it seems. Those cat-shifting aliens won't know what hit them!

DRAGONLINGS OF VALDIER NOVELLAS

The Valdier, Sarafin, and Curizan Lords had children who just cannot stop getting into trouble! There is nothing as cute or funny as magical, shapeshifting kids, and nothing as heartwarming as family.

COSMOS' GATEWAY

Cosmos created a portal between his lab and the warriors of Prime. Discover new worlds, new species, and outrageous adventures as secrets are unraveled and bridges are crossed.

THE ALLIANCE

When Earth received its first visitors from space, the planet was thrown into a panicked chaos. The Trivators came to bring Earth into the Alliance of Star Systems, but now they must take control to prevent the humans from destroying themselves. No one was prepared for how the humans will affect the Trivators, though, starting with a family of three sisters....

LORDS OF KASSIS

It began with a random abduction and a stowaway, and yet, somehow, the Kassisans knew the humans were coming long before now. The fate of more than one world hangs in the balance, and time is not always linear....

ZION WARRIORS

Time travel, epic heroics, and love beyond measure. Sci-fi adventures with heart and soul, laughter, and awe-inspiring discovery...

Paranormal / Fantasy / Romance

MAGIC, NEW MEXICO

Within New Mexico is a small town named Magic, an... unusual town, to say the least. With no beginning and no end, spanning genres, authors, and universes, hilarity and drama combine to keep you on the edge of your seat!

SPIRIT PASS

There is a physical connection between two times. Follow the stories of those who *travel back and forth. These westerns are as wild as they come!*

Second Chance

Stand-alone worlds featuring a woman who remembers her own death. Fiery and mysterious, these books will steal your heart.

More Than Human

Long ago there was a war on Earth between shifters and humans. Humans lost, and today they know they will become extinct if something is not done....

The Fairy Tale Series

A twist on your favorite fairy tales!

A Seven Kingdoms Tale

Long ago, a strange entity came to the Seven Kingdoms to conquer and feed on their life force. It found a host, and she battled it within her body for centuries while destruction and devastation surrounded her. Our story begins when the end is near, and a portal is opened....

Epic Science Fiction / Action Thrillers

Project Gliese 581G

An international team leave Earth to investigate a mysterious object in our solar system that was clearly made by someone, someone who isn't from Earth. Discover new worlds and conflicts in a sci-fi adventure sure to become your favorite!

New Adult / Young Adult

Breaking Free

A journey that will challenge everything she has ever believed about herself as danger reveals itself in sudden, heart-stopping moments.

The Dust Series

Fragments of a comet hit Earth, and Dust wakes to discover the world as he knew it is gone. It isn't the only thing that has changed, though, so has Dust...

ABOUT THE AUTHOR

S.E. Smith is an *internationally acclaimed, New York Times* **and** *USA TODAY Bestselling* author of science fiction, romance, fantasy, paranormal, and contemporary works for adults, young adults, and children. She enjoys writing a wide variety of genres that pull her readers into worlds that take them away.

www.ingramcontent.com/pod-product-compliance
Lightning Source LLC
Chambersburg PA
CBHW051924220626
47052CB00003B/561